D1379832

SPECIAL MESSAGE TO READERS

This book is published under the auspices of

THE ULVERSCROFT FOUNDATION

(registered charity No. 264873 UK)

Established in 1972 to provide funds for research, diagnosis and treatment of eye diseases. Examples of contributions made are: —

A Children's Assessment Unit at Moorfield's Hospital, London.

•

Twin operating theatres at the Western Ophthalmic Hospital, London.

•

A Chair of Ophthalmology at the Royal Australian College of Ophthalmologists.

•

The Ulverscroft Children's Eye Unit at the Great Ormond Street Hospital For Sick Children, London.

You can help further the work of the Foundation by making a donation or leaving a legacy. Every contribution, no matter how small, is received with gratitude. Please write for details to:

THE ULVERSCROFT FOUNDATION,
The Green, Bradgate Road, Anstey,
Leicester LE7 7FU, England.
Telephone: (0116) 236 4325

In Australia write to:

THE ULVERSCROFT FOUNDATION,
c/o The Royal Australian and New Zealand College of Ophthalmologists,
94-98 Chalmers Street, Surry Hills,
N.S.W. 2010, Australia

SCARE TACTICS

These seven short stories take you on a trip through the twilight world of the supernatural, which include: the terrifying universe where men fall in love with monsters; a troubled child's nightmares which prove to be real; a house which attracts evil much as a sponge attracts water; and demons, from a time before history, making Satanic pacts in order to return from the past. Not a journey for the faint-hearted — there will be no shortage of scare tactics.

Books by David Whitehead
in the Linford Mystery Library:

THE FLUTTERING

DAVID WHITEHEAD

SCARE TACTICS

Complete and Unabridged

LINFORD
Leicester

First published in Great Britain

First Linford Edition
published 2009

British Library CIP Data

Whitehead, David, *1958* –
Scare tactics.- -(Linford mystery library)
1. Occult fiction, English.
2. Large type books.
I. Title II. Series
823.9′14–dc22

ISBN 978–1–84782–943–6

Published by
F. A. Thorpe (Publishing)
Anstey, Leicestershire

Set by Words & Graphics Ltd.
Anstey, Leicestershire
Printed and bound in Great Britain by
T. J. International Ltd., Padstow, Cornwall

This book is printed on acid-free paper

In Memory of
Chick

Contents

Empty-Handed

I

When Stewart finished searching all the obvious places and still couldn't find the safe, he started looking in all the *not*-so-obvious ones, and that was when he heard the crunch and hiss of tyres on gravel, and car headlamps filled the room with a shifting half-light.

The pattern of the curtains slid silently across the walls, delicate lace flowers scuttling like fat, agitated insects over the grotesque wooden masks and book-stuffed shelves. Then the car engine died, the headlamps went off, and shadows settled again like black silk over the room.

Stewart froze, telling himself that it was most probably someone paying a surprise visit, unaware that the house was empty.

He stood in the centre of the study, a youngish, thick-set, hard-faced man in a worn motorcycle jacket and baggy jeans, staring fixedly into the darkness as he sought to catch every sound.

A car door slammed, footsteps crackled on stone and then there was nothing but silence again.

He tensed. It couldn't be Palmer coming back, not this early. Every Friday evening for the past three weeks he'd watched Palmer leave the house at eight and return home at one or two the following morning. Wherever he went, it was obviously a regular thing.

No, he told himself, it's not Palmer. It *can't* be. It's just someone hoping to catch him at home.

But then Stewart's keen ears picked up the sound of a key turning in the front door lock, and he had to fight a sudden urge to panic.

He crossed to the door and opened it just a crack. From here he could see the hallway below, the oblong of frosty moonlight as the front door swung open, the stretched shadow of Richard Palmer oozing inside, and Palmer himself closing the door behind him.

A sharp click snapped the silence, and

light filled the hallway. He heard Palmer's footsteps, muffled by thick carpet, and quietly closed the door again, his mind racing.

It was possible that Palmer had just popped back quickly because he'd forgotten something. He *could* be going straight out again.

But then he heard more sounds: another light being switched on and the gentle clatter of fine china, and he thought with a mixture of anger and disbelief, *The bastard's making himself a cup of tea!*

Stewart swore softly. What the hell was he supposed to do *now?*

He sat on the edge of the large, leather-topped desk, setting his weight down gently so that it wouldn't creak, and forced his knotted muscles to relax. Like it or not, there was nothing he could do but wait. After all, anything could have happened. Maybe Palmer wasn't feeling well and would shortly go to bed. Maybe. That was Stewart's best bet. Palmer would have to be in bed or in the shower before he could chance retracing his steps through the house, out through the patio doors and across to the seven-foot high brick wall at the far end of the garden.

From there it would be a short jog through the dead autumn leaves until he reached the little pocket of shrubbery where he'd left his old Suzuki Marauder. Then he would gun the engine and drive away, and nobody would know he'd ever been there.

But . . .

Again he swore softly.

You only had to look at Palmer's home — a large, Tudor-style property set in the Hertfordshire countryside — to see that the man was loaded. He was a top London publisher, he drove a big car, was seen in all the best places with all the right people. He was just begging to be ripped off.

But you couldn't stay out tonight, could you, you bastard!

Stewart's hands, encased in thin disposable gloves, folded into hard-knuckled fists, and his teeth clamped in a sudden, fiery rage. He hated to leave a place empty-handed, always had, but what else could he do?

Oh, sure, he could wait until Palmer went to bed and then continue his search for the safe, but he preferred to have a place to himself when he worked. Besides, he couldn't take even the slightest chance of getting caught now. He'd only been out of nick for a month as it was!

The thought made him realise just what a fix he was in.

More lights were being switched on or off downstairs. As he eased the study door open again, classical music floated up to him, and he blew a hard breath.

Well, that was that, then. It sounded like Palmer was properly settled in for the night.

Stewart's palms turned clammy and all at once his nerve began to slip. *Me*, he thought. *Christ, I must be getting old. There was a time when* nothing *would've fazed me*.

But the memory of eighteen months in prison now began to squeeze gently at his chest, and the prospect of going down again, this time for three years, minimum, made it even more difficult to breathe.

He tried to fight it, but all at once the desperation flooded out of him and he screamed silently, *I've got to get out of here!*

But how?

How?

He opened the study door and stepped cautiously out onto the landing, where he moved to the head of the stairs and peered down. There was no movement, just the music and the lights to show that Palmer had come home.

His eyes travelled along the hallway. If he could just make it downstairs and out the front door . . .

All right, so Palmer would know he'd had a visitor, but that didn't matter. He wouldn't be able to give the police a description, that was the main thing. By the time *he* came running, Stewart would be out of the house and swallowed up by the night.

It was risky, of course. But so was hanging about up here, waiting for Palmer to come upstairs and catch him.

Again he considered the front door,

chewing on his bottom lip. Then, like a diver about to go under, he sucked in a deep breath and gently set his weight down on the top step.

He made no sound in the rich carpet.

The music, now dark and ominous like an approaching storm, drifted up to him from the lounge.

He moved down to the next step, then the next, his unblinking gaze fixed on the half-open lounge doorway.

He took another step. *Not far to go now*, he told himself.

And then the lights went out.

His first thought was that it was a power cut. But no, it *couldn't* be a power cut, because the music was still play —

All at once the lights came back on, and he thought he heard footsteps below. Immediately he retraced his steps, slipped back into the study and closed the door behind him.

Hiding in the darkness, he battled to calm his increasingly erratic breathing. If he started hyperventilating now, he was finished for sure.

In a desperate attempt to distract

himself, he pressed an ear to the door and listened. Nothing. Perhaps Palmer had gone to check his fuse box.

Stewart forced himself to relax a little. Maybe he could try again in a minute.

But then, so abruptly that the knowledge hit him like a jab in the belly, he realised that he was no longer alone in the room, and even as he spun around, the Anglepoise lamp on the desk snapped on, stabbing him with its beam.

Instinctively Stewart brought his right hand up, partly to shield his eyes from the glare, partly to hide his face behind a dark, fingers-and-thumb shadow.

On the walls, the masks developed shadowy pits for eyes.

And behind the desk stood Palmer

II

He was of average height and cadaverous build, and his hair was as completely black as his deep-set eyes. He had a long, thin, clean-shaven face that was disturbingly asexual, with a small, almost delicate mouth and a sharp hatchet-blade nose. He was in his late fifties, but in the poor light it was hard to say whether or not he looked it.

He pulled an exclusive Rocco LeTrey scarf from around his neck, shrugged out of an equally expensive topcoat and threw them both carelessly onto his chair. Then, very deliberately, he peeled a pair of black leather Takara Tsukiko gloves from his pale hands and let them drop onto the coat, his eyes never once leaving Stewart's face.

His Rolex and assorted rings glittered richly as he folded his arms across his narrow chest.

For a moment they stood facing each other. Then Stewart turned and reached for the door handle. The game was up. All that mattered now was to get out of here before Palmer got a good enough look at him to give his description to the police.

But Palmer's voice halted him in his tracks.

'I've been expecting you,' he said.

Freezing, Stewart was drawn to look at him again from behind one upraised hand.

'Not *you* personally,' Palmer clarified. 'But someone *like* you.' He glanced around the room. 'It's this house, isn't it?' he noted conversationally. 'Big and secluded. People like you can't *resist* it.'

Stewart didn't like the sound of that. It made the place seem like some sort of bait. He turned and grabbed the door handle again, but the door wouldn't open. He pulled at it with such force that the masks shivered against the walls, but it must've stuck in the frame.

Behind him, he heard Palmer slip a top-of-the-range cell phone from an inside jacket pocket and thumb in a number.

Three digits.

'Hello? Yes, the police, please.'

The words brought pearls of sweat to Stewart's forehead. He tugged at the door again but it was stuck fast. *Locked?* His eyes fell to the handle. There was no keyhole, it *couldn't* be locked.

Behind him, Palmer said, 'Yes, I'd like to report an attempted burglary.'

Stewart pushed himself away from the door and spun around, the skin stretching tight across his skull. In three strides he was across to the desk, where he tore the phone from Palmer's fist and flung it across the room.

It shattered with a vicious snap.

In the silence that followed, their eyes locked until Stewart twisted the Anglepoise away from him. His rubber-clad fists clenched and he drew his right hand back in a threatening gesture, but Palmer showed no fear. If anything, there seemed to be a challenge in his dark eyes, almost as if he was *daring* Stewart to strike him. But all Stewart said was, 'Open the door.'

Palmer smiled as though faintly amused by him, and raised one eyebrow.

‘I said open the fucking *door!*’ Stewart snarled. He drew his fist further back as a warning, not sure if he would actually strike the publisher or not.

‘It isn’t locked,’ Palmer said softly.

As Stewart studied him, he thought, *Christ, I’ve made a right balls-up of this. He’s seen me. I mean, he’s* really *seen me*. ‘It won’t open,’ he muttered. ‘It must be stuck or something.’

Palmer chuckled. ‘You’ll have to excuse me,’ he said. ‘It’s just that a burglar who can’t open an unlocked door must be something of a rarity in your profession.’

Stewart frowned. ‘What’s up with you? Aren’t you scared?’

‘*Should* I be?’

Stewart didn’t know the answer to that one himself. He moved back to the door, not once taking his eyes off the publisher. He felt for the handle, turned it. Still the door was jammed in the frame. He yanked at it, but it did no good.

Quietly, almost in defeat, he muttered, ‘What have you done to it?’

‘Me?’

'Yes, *you*,' Stewart barked. 'It was all right just now.'

'I never touched it.'

'Then how the fuck did you get in here?'

Again, that faint lift of an eyebrow.

'How did you even know I was *up* here?'

But Palmer was busily inspecting the phone Stewart had thrown across the room, turning the two pieces between his long fingers as if they were rare jewels. He'd moved around the desk and across the room with all the sound of a shadow. 'Have you any idea how much these things cost?' he asked with mild irritation.

Stewart wanted to hit him now, and go *on* hitting him, but somehow he held back. Instead he demanded, 'How did you get past me on the stairs?'

Palmer moved back around the desk. He gave no sign of having heard Stewart's question, but asked one of his own. 'What is your name?'

Stewart laughed harshly. 'Come off it.'

'What is it?'

'Smith.'

Palmer nodded. 'As you wish, Mr . . . *Smith*.'

He studied Stewart closely for a long, thoughtful moment, then murmured, '*I wonder* . . . '

He said no more for a while, then finally broke his silence again with, 'We have ourselves a very interesting situation here, Mr Smith. Very interesting, and quite possibly very fortuitous — for *both* of us.'

Stewart said nothing.

'You are in very serious trouble,' Palmer reminded him. 'Caught red-handed, as they say. But I am not an uncharitable man. Why should I exercise my right to make a citizen's arrest, when I could just as easily allow you to go free? To give you a chance to *earn* your freedom?'

Sensing a possible lifeline, Stewart asked hesitantly, 'What would I have to do? You're not gay, are you?'

'No.'

'How would I earn it, then?'

Palmer said softly, 'By killing someone for me.'

III

There was an instant of absolute silence before Stewart finally released his pent-up breath in a rush.

'Is this some kind of joke?' he asked. 'That how you get your jollies, is it, fucking with other people's minds?'

'Hear me out,' replied the publisher, leaning forward into the pale light. 'And know this, Smith: that I am deadly serious about this proposition. *Deadly* serious.'

He straightened again, giving his words a chance to sink in.

'There is, of course, more to it than you need to know,' he continued. 'However, if it makes the thing any easier for you, the man I want you to kill *deserves* to die. He is evil. He has power and influence, and unless he is stopped he will gain more. Too much. To maintain a balance of sanity, he *must* be stopped.'

To buy himself more time, Stewart asked, 'What is he, a politician, or something?'

Palmer hesitated. 'What he is needn't concern you. All that matters is that he must *die*.'

Stewart shook his head. 'You've got the wrong man, mate. I might be a lot of things, but I'm not a killer.'

Palmer's black eyes glittered. 'And as you can see, I am not a poor man. For a job well done I can afford to be . . . generous.'

There was something in the way he said the word that stirred all the greed Stewart had ever known.

'In addition to your freedom,' said Palmer, 'I will see to it that you are adequately rewarded.'

There was a long silence. At last Stewart asked, 'Why do you want him dead?'

'I've already told you.'

'You've told me sod all. Why do you want him dead?'

Palmer allowed himself an elaborate

sigh. 'He is part of a very powerful . . . association. If he were to become its leader, I believe he would twist its power to serve his own ends.'

'An association?' Stewart repeated. 'He's a businessman, you mean?'

'Something like that.'

Stewart said, very definitely, 'You're lying.'

Their eyes met and locked in the half-light. Stewart made a sound of impatience. The crazy old bastard had almost got him then, with all his talk of murder and reward. He tried to open the study door again, but still it wouldn't budge.

'Very well,' Palmer hissed as he came around the desk. 'The truth.

'For want of a better description, the man I want you to kill is a high priest in the cult of Milaroth. An ambitious man, a *ruthless* man, he intends to force me out and seize the leadership for himself. But it was *I* who formed the cult in the first place, and it is *I* who should sit at Milaroth's right hand! I tell you, Smith, he is a very dangerous individual. *I* can lead our cult to glory, but *he* can only bring it down around our ears!'

He calmed himself only with effort, and when his breathing regulated, he said, 'Now, when he is . . . removed . . . I must have an alibi that is beyond reproach. If I am suspected of having any connection with his death, I will lose my standing among my fellow worshippers, otherwise I would gladly do the job myself.

'If *you* do this thing on my behalf, you can have everything you've ever desired. If not . . . '

Stewart snorted. 'You're off your rocker, mate.'

Palmer shook his head. 'No, Mr . . . ' His eyes closed for a moment, and the lids quivered visibly. Then he smiled slightly and said, 'Mr *Stewart*.'

Stewart's eyes bugged.

'If it will help to convince you,' Palmer went on, 'allow me to perform a simple example of my power. The power of Milaroth.'

His black eyes focused on a point beyond Stewart's shoulder and he waved his right hand briefly across his chest as he muttered a strange, dead word of one syllable. Then he nodded to the door.

'Open it.'

Stewart glanced briefly at the door, afraid to take his eyes off Palmer for any length of time now. He reached out and took hold of the handle. It felt slightly warm beneath his grip. When the door itself opened freely, the breath hitched in his throat.

Behind him, Palmer was smiling again.

Stewart knew he should grab the opportunity to run, but still he hesitated. Palmer had somehow discovered his name. What *else* did he know? Oh, the old bastard was crazy, sure. But that just made him all the more dangerous.

Thoughtfully he swung the door back and forth. It moved soundlessly on perfectly balanced hinges. At no time had it been wedged in the frame.

And that was another thing. How had Palmer gotten past him on the stairs? He remembered the lights blinking off for a second or so, but hardly long enough for a grown man to move silently up a flight of stairs and right past him, unnoticed.

Could it be that there was something to all this talk of cults and magic after all?

'Why don't you get this Mila-whatsit to do your dirty work for you?' he asked, almost before he realised he was speaking.

Palmer made a sound in his throat. 'Such matters are beneath him,' he replied. 'Milaroth conserves his strength for the day of his rebirth.'

Stewart shrugged. 'All right. Let's suppose all this is on the level. Why pressure *me* into doing the job? If you're willing to pay out so much to get it done, why not hire a professional?'

'Don't think I haven't considered it. I probably *would* have if you hadn't come along. But you're here. And there have been certain . . . developments . . . tonight which require me to act quickly.'

Stewart nodded. Suddenly he started to feel better about this thing, more in control of the situation. 'Suppose I say I'll do it, then. How do I know you won't double-cross me?'

'Because I will give you a substantial advance — in cash — as a sign of my goodwill. Plus your freedom, of course.'

'And what's to stop *me* from double-crossing *you?*'

Something in Palmer's eyes frosted over. 'Let's just say that I wouldn't . . . *advise* it.'

He cocked his head to one side. 'Now,' he said. 'I ask you again. If you enter into our bargain, you will be amply rewarded. If not . . . well, there are some things better left . . . unsaid.'

Behind him, quite deliberately, the door closed with a gentle click. When he tried to open it, Stewart again found it stuck fast. He turned to Palmer, who was now resting against the desk exactly the way *he* had, a lifetime before.

'Well?'

'You're crazy,' Stewart whispered.

'And impatient. *Well?*'

Greed wanted him to accept and damn the consequences, but fear made him say, 'Stick it.'

Abruptly he turned back to the door and aimed a heavy kick at the handle. He'd take his chances outside. He had a couple of mates who'd swear blind he was with them all evening. And what if the

Old Bill *did* give him a tug? There was no evidence against him, only Palmer's word that he'd ever been there.

'It won't do you any good, you know.'

Stewart spun around to face the publisher again, jabbing a finger at the door. '*Open it!*' he yelled.

He took two steps forward, his large fists raised, but still the publisher just stood there, mouth thinned, arms folded, unafraid.

'I'll make that phone call, shall I?' he asked.

Pulling up sharp, Stewart glanced down and whispered, '*What . . . ?*'

The cell phone in Palmer's hand, the cracked, broken, dead cell phone, was whole once more.

Whole, and working.

IV

Palmer keyed in two of the three numbers before Stewart slapped him hard across the face. The publisher went back, the phone dropping to the floor. Stewart grabbed him around the throat and forced him back onto the desktop, and Palmer's computer screen, keyboard, an ashtray, a Filofax, a pot filled with pens and pencils, they all spilled back over his discarded coat and gloves as Stewart clasped his throat shut.

'*Open the door!*'

Palmer wriggled beneath him like a landed fish, his arms swiping back and forth to land a series of ineffectual blows against Stewart's rigid arms. His eyes shone with fear and his skin began to darken.

'*Do you understand me?*' Stewart bellowed. '*Open it!*'

Palmer managed a desperate, restricted nod. 'All . . . right . . . all right . . . '

Behind him, Stewart heard the door click open. He held his strangling grip for a moment more until his rage subsided, then pushed himself away from the publisher.

'You're a fucking *nutter*,' he rasped.

He turned away and took one step toward the door before he sensed movement behind him.

Wheeling back, he saw Palmer thrusting himself away from the desk. In his right hand he held an ornate letter opener, and in his face there was murder.

Without even thinking about it, Stewart grabbed Palmer's wrist with his left hand even as his right bunched and drove forward. The impact of his fist against Palmer's jaw was hard: harder than he'd intended. The publisher's head snapped sideways, and a loud, dry crack of breaking bone filled the room. Palmer dropped the letter opener, stood there a moment longer, then collapsed.

His mouth opened and closed as he tried to use his last rattling breaths to frame some words, and his eyes took on a weird, wide look as they flicked about the room. They settled at last, as Stewart knew they must, on him, and raked his face for stretched seconds: two reptilian eyes that held onto life even as the rest of him lay dying.

Then the eyes slid away from him and settled on a spot beyond the desk, where everything from the desk had landed in a heap around his chair. He managed two, perhaps three words. It was difficult to know where one ended and another began, since they weren't in any language Stewart had ever heard before. Only then did the light dim in his eyes, and with one final, shuddering breath, he died.

For a long while Stewart stared down at the corpse, his fists slowly unbuckling. Then he took a quick, guilty step away from the body. *Get the hell out*, he told himself. *Get the hell out of here* . . .

He took another backward step, realised the door was slowly closing again and quickly flung himself out onto the landing an instant before it slammed shut.

He fell to his knees, shivering. For the next few seconds he was lost in a confusion of shock and panic, until a cool breeze stroked his face. Then he gave a high, mad giggle.

A draught had blown the door shut, nothing else. No spirits or spells, just a draught!

Almost immediately, however, he sobered. There was a dead body on the other side of that door, and he was responsible for it. He had to get out, quick.

But damn it, he hated to leave a place empty-handed!

He studied the door for a long moment. If Palmer kept anything of real value in the house, Stewart felt certain it would be in the study. He knew for sure it wasn't anywhere else.

Anything would do. Anything was better than nothing. Remembering the way Palmer's rings and watch had glittered, he felt another sensual caress of greed.

Getting to his feet, he paused, trying to find the courage to reach out and twist the door handle. *Leave well enough alone*, whispered a cautionary voice inside him.

But . . .

He opened the door.

The first thing he saw was the body on the floor. It lay cold and still, its skin faintly blue in the overturned light of the Anglepoise. He licked his lips, then took a step into the room.

Nothing stirred.

He grabbed a few of the musty old books from the nearest shelf and stacked them against the door in case it should blow shut again. Then he took another step into the room.

He let his breath out in a heavy sigh.

There, that's better. Nothing to be afraid of.

In a moment he was crouching by the body and easing the rings from Palmer's lifeless fingers.

He was just working on the third one when a faint scratching sound made him jump. He stood up quickly, his eyes shooting to a spot behind the desk, where he thought the noise had come from.

He saw nothing.

After a pause his eyes fell back to Palmer's jewellery, unease still making his skin crawl.

He tore the Rolex from Palmer's cold wrist, stuffed it into his pocket and turned toward the door. The scratching noise came again and he spun around, half expecting the dead publisher to sit up and smile at him.

But Palmer lay where he was, and Stewart's eyes caught a flash of movement just beyond the light of the desk lamp — something dark that scuttled across the floor.

He let his breath out in a sigh of relief. *Mice*, he thought. *For all his finery, the old bastard had mice*.

He turned and took two steps toward the door.

Then the stack of books overbalanced and slid across his path.

The door slammed shut.

The desk lamp went out.

He gave a frightened yelp as he leapt for the door. His fingers strangled the handle, but the door was stuck again.

Stuck?

He turned quickly, put his back to the wall, heard the scratching noise again, nearer this time. But he wasn't afraid of mice.

No. It's Palmer's dead body I'm afraid of.

In his mind he saw Palmer's bright black eyes slipping away to stare at something beyond the desk, heard the two or three arcane words he'd muttered before he died, remembered Palmer saying, *Some things are better left . . . unsaid*.

The scampering came from somewhere close to his right. He strained to penetrate the darkness but couldn't see a thing. His hand slid up the wall to the light switch. He flicked it but nothing happened.

Again he thought of Palmer's body.

Cautiously he moved away from the wall, turned and felt for the handle of the door. When he had it pinpointed, he stepped back and kicked at it with the sole of his boot. He didn't know whether or not it would do any good, but he had to do *something* before his frayed nerves snapped altogether.

He kicked again.

Once more.

He aimed a fourth kick.

And then a hand closed around his ankle.

V

His cry split the silence. It was Palmer. He *knew* it was Palmer! The mad bastard wasn't dead after all!

He lashed out with his foot, trying to catch the publisher in the face, but his foot cut only the empty air.

The hand grasping his ankle gave a tug and he fell. Pain jarred through the small of his back. He kicked at his ankle with the other heel, hoping to loosen the hand holding it, but more pain exploded in his leg and he realised that the hand had let go.

He rolled over and sprang up, reaching for the door. He was yelling curses now, trying to work himself into a temper so that fury would replace fear. He pulled at the door even as the scampering grew closer in the blackness behind him.

Without warning the door flew open

and he fell back into the shadows, regained his balance and then threw himself out onto the landing again. He struck the far wall with a force that shook the paintings hanging there: then, without looking back, he raced for the stairs.

He was halfway down when, in his haste, he tripped.

The heavy crash he made hitting the stairs sounded worse than it actually was, but even so pain tore through him and the world became a tumbling, twisting kaleidoscope of walls, carpets and ceiling, until he rolled off the bottom stair and sprawled on his back, dazed and aching.

Before he could properly recover, there came a series of dull thuds on the stairs above him. Someone was coming down after him!

Palmer!

He forced himself up onto his knees, ignoring the aches that dug into his bruised bones, expecting to see the publisher looking down at him with one eyebrow raised to see what Stewart thought of his latest trick: of coming back from the dead.

Allow me to perform a simple example of my power. The power of Milaroth.

He did not expect to see Palmer's two black Takara Tsukiko gloves.

They flopped from one step to the next, the leather looking more like damp black skin as the empty fingers twitched and flexed and continued to propel them forward.

Fear held him frozen for vital seconds as he continued to watch their descent through glassy eyes. This could *not* be happening. But after what he'd already seen tonight, he wasn't prepared to take the chance that he was just imagining it. With a strangled cry he leapt back to his feet and lurched toward the front door.

Behind him, one of the gloves dropped to the floor and began to scuttle after him.

A spell, Stewart thought wildly. *He cast a spell*. Those dead words he muttered were *a spell!*

His hand closed around the handle and he pulled, half expecting to find the door wedged in the frame. But it wasn't wedged.

It was *locked*.

And bolted.

The keys! Where're the keys?

He spun around, his eyes dropping to the approaching glove-thing. Sweat washed down his face as he watched the busy fingers driving it ever closer.

This can't be happening! his mind screamed at him. *It can't be!*

But he knew with gut-twisting certainty that it *was* happening. As incredible as it was, it *was* happening.

Trying to swallow his revulsion, he stepped forward and brought his foot down on the advancing glove. It flattened beneath his heel as if it had been filled with nothing more substantial than air. But when he lifted his foot again it seemed to reinflate and continue thrusting toward him, its questing black fingers flexing eagerly as they sought him out.

He sidestepped the glove and hurled himself along the hallway, thinking, *Right into the dining room, out through the patio doors —*

The second glove fell onto his shoulder.

He gave a yell and brushed it off, but

even as it fell to the floor and neatly flipped back onto its spider's-leg fingers, the first glove grabbed his ankle again. He kicked at it but it wouldn't loosen its grip.

He ran a few more steps and burst into the dining room, but by then the second glove had grabbed his other ankle, and together they hauled backward.

Stewart crashed forward, striking his head on the edge of the dining table before hitting the floor. Warm blood splashed from a gash in his forehead, but his cries were muffled by the pile of the carpet.

Dimly he felt the weight of the gloves as they scuttled up his legs and across his back. Desperately fighting to remain conscious, he tried to push himself to his feet, but the gloves stopped their advance and spread out, palms flat against his shoulder blades.

When they shoved him back against the carpet the wind was knocked out of him and little flashes of light popped before his eyes.

Then the gloves continued their upward climb.

He tried to roll over and crush them with his body, but terror had cramped his muscles and he realised vaguely that the fall had concussed him and his coordination was shot to hell.

When the gloves finally closed around his throat, the leather had the moist, sticky feel of long-dead skin. He cried out again, still fighting to rise, but the hands that weren't hands at all continued to squeeze tighter and tighter, and try as he might, he couldn't seem to tear them away.

There was nothing to . . . grip . . . onto . . . nothing . . . at . . . alllll . . .

⋆ ⋆ ⋆

When his legs finally stopped kicking and his face was almost black, the gloves loosened their grip on his throat and paused momentarily, as if to satisfy themselves that he really *was* dead and not just pretending.

Eventually they climbed down off his body and scampered away like two odd but eager young children.

Nothing else stirred in the secluded, Tudor-style house. There was no sound now but the ticking of expensive clocks and the faint buzz of the refrigerator in the kitchen.

In the study, Palmer lay cold and dead. In the dining room, Stewart lay much the same way. After a few days, the bodies began to smell.

The gloves were never seen again.

Imbued with a life of their own, they had left the house for pastures new.

Furthermore, they left . . . *empty-handed*.

Once Bitten

Edwards was on the motorway when the fog came down. It fell as a thick grey blanket that quickly smothered the milky November sunshine, and brought with it a moist, penetrating chill that could be felt even in the car.

That's all I need, Edwards told himself peevishly, glancing at the clock on the dashboard. It was a little after two. Well, so much for getting to Reading on time. The meeting would be over and done with by the time *he* got there.

He checked his mirrors, switched on his headlights and window wipers, dropped back to a little over twenty and then lit another cigarette to calm his rising temper.

Five minutes later he felt the first faint stirrings of nausea and thought dimly, *Not again*.

As usual, it started as a flush of warmth that turned his skin a blotchy red, and then an ugly lump appeared in his throat that made him want to puke. He swallowed with effort, fumbled open the window and tried to take his mind off his churning guts by concentrating on his driving. Cold air rushed in to dry the sweat on his face.

The sickness decided him. Reading could wait. In fact, as far as he was concerned right then, Reading could wait *permanently*.

His mind made up, he left the motorway at the next exit and pulled over about a mile later, when he found himself in a wide, misty lane flanked by tall, bare elms. Switching on his hazards, he sat back and closed his eyes. His heart was still hammering, but he felt better because he'd finally reached a decision about something that had been bugging him for long enough. He was getting out of this business once and for all.

He wasn't cut out to be a manager, that was the thing. At first, what with the extra money and the company Avensis, he'd thought it was a chance in a million, to go up through the ranks from pest control serviceman to area manager.

But there had been more to it than that, of course. There was all the extra paperwork, for a start. The sales targets he never seemed able to meet. Having to keep up to date on ever-changing health and safety requirements. Stock-checks, call-outs, call-*backs*, chasing the men to make sure they met their own targets because if they didn't, it was *him*, Kevin Edwards, who'd get it in the neck. And of course, the bi-monthly area manager's meetings, always held in Reading.

I ask you, he thought. *Fucking Reading!*

He felt the vomit rising again then, and hurriedly opened the car door. Even as he leaned sideways, it boiled up into his throat and burst from between his twisted lips in a chunky torrent. He screwed his eyes shut and made a weird kind of grunting sound, and despite the chill he grew so hot in those few wretched seconds that he thought he might actually start to melt.

Then the feeling faded, and he became aware of his pounding heart again, his laboured breathing, the sweat turning cold against his flushed skin. He shivered, sat back, shut the door again. He was shaking.

Ten minutes later he got out of the car and walked slowly up and down the verge to get some air and hopefully hasten his recovery. The lane was quiet now. Everything was quiet. With no breeze to disperse it, the fog simply hung in the freezing air, seeming to pulse faintly to the rhythm of his blinking hazards.

He took out another cigarette, lit it and drew smoke into his lungs. Somewhere out in the murk a bird made a lonely, cawing sound. It reminded him of his own isolation.

Glancing idly at the trees, he thought, *Funny, some of the things that stick in the mind*.

He'd read once that the elm was the tree of melancholy and death, mostly because its branches had a tendency to fall without warning: that, and the fact that elm had once been the principal wood from which coffins were made.

Cheerful, he told himself dryly.

He was just finishing the cigarette when the fog coasted gently away from a previously-hidden sign about fifteen metres ahead. It pointed the way to a place called Maplewick.

Edwards' eyes narrowed at the name. It sounded vaguely familiar, although he was sure he'd never been there before. Still, it was bound to have a pub, and since he wasn't going to make it to Reading now . . .

The fog closed in again and the sign vanished from view.

Running a palm across his slippery face, he got back into the car, took out his phone and called the Reading office.

'Hello, Julie? Yeah, it's Kev. Listen, I'm not going to make it . . . Well, I'm stuck in fog, for a start . . . Thick? Listen, love, it's so thick you could sew a button on it . . . No, I'm not gonna get there. Any case, I'm feeling a bit rough . . . I don't know, the flu, I think. Yeah. I'm going to find a place to pull over till it lifts, might get my head down if I can and sleep it off . . . No, it'll be all right.'

He ended the call, squared his

shoulders, started the engine and set off again, passing the sign at a careful crawl and then taking the next left.

Now that he thought about it, he realised that he *had* been through this way once before, but that had been well over a year ago and he couldn't remember much about it now.

About twenty minutes later he drove past an ornate village sign and what he took to be a village green, and kept going. He passed the first of the cottages without even seeing them: then the fog thinned ever so slightly, and at last the dark, narrow shapes of half-timbered houses with steep, red-tiled roofs became visible.

He could just about make out the sky again, too. It was a deep, evening blue. The clock on the dashboard said it was a quarter to five, but it might just as well have been midnight. There were no streetlights. Only the icy rising of the full moon provided any illumination.

Maplewick High Street meandered gently uphill, a tight, cobbled thoroughfare flanked on either side by picturesque but cramped and crooked-looking medieval cottages with tiny, mullioned windows. No two were alike, but all had their curtains drawn against the early evening.

The street itself was empty.

He drove a little faster now, scanning both sides for a pub, hotel or guest-house. Within six minutes, however, he was back at the village green. Somehow he'd driven in a complete circle.

He pulled over and killed the engine. There was nothing for it but to knock at one of the cottages and ask for directions.

He climbed out of the car, his breath condensing in the damp air, and had just started crossing the road when something came rushing out of the fog and knocked him to the ground.

He cried out in surprise and immediately started struggling with his assailant, who had landed on top of him. A frantic moment later he leapt back to his feet and spotted a bicycle lying on its side, back wheel still spinning.

The thing he'd just thrown off was getting up again, only now he saw that it was a man.

To be more precise, it was a *police*man.

Edwards thought, *Oh Christ*, and said hurriedly, 'Hey, I'm sorry, mate. Are you all right . . . ?'

The policeman straightened up. He was a tall, heavy-set man in his late fifties, with a cheerful, bearded face and friendly blue eyes. 'It's me as should be apologisin',' he replied breathlessly. 'On account it was me who ran into *you*.'

He brushed at his tunic and fussed with his tie. 'Sorry 'bout that,' he went on. 'Silly as it sounds, I di'n't see you till the last minute. Too busy wonderin' what the missus has got for me tea, I 'spect.'

Edwards smiled obligingly.

'Any case,' the policeman continued, retrieving his bike and giving it a quick once-over, 'the streets is usually empty this time o' th'evenin'. Don't get too many visitors 'round here, even on a good day. But you'm not a visitor, I'll bet. You prob'ly took a wrong turn in this fog an' want directions back to the motorway.'

'Actually, I was looking for a place to stay the night,' Edwards corrected him.

'A place to stay the night, eh?' repeated

the policeman. He thought for a moment, as if this tiny hamlet had so many places to choose from. 'Have you tried the pub?'

'I haven't even managed to *find* the pub, yet,' Edwards replied ruefully.

'Well, go on up th'High Street, here, an' take your first right into Copper Kettle Lane. Follow Copper Kettle Lane right to the very bottom an' you'll come to the pub. You can't miss it. Old Albert should be able to fix you up.'

'Thanks.'

When the policeman had gone on his way, Edwards climbed back into the car. He wasn't sure it was worth staying the night now that the fog had more or less lifted. Perhaps he should just head back to London, phone in sick for a couple of days and use the time to consider his options.

But he'd had enough of travelling for one day, and it certainly wouldn't do him any harm to spend a night away from his lonely bedsit. He'd phone the office first thing in the morning, then get an early start back, be in London a little after nine and in the Jobcentre by ten.

He found Copper Kettle Lane easily enough, and followed it for about half a mile or so until it opened onto another dark and seemingly deserted country lane. On the far side of the road stood a long, pink building with a terracotta-red roof and a sign above the central door which identified it as *The Hair of the Dog*. Edwards drove across the road and into the small gravel car park beside it.

When he finally let himself inside, the pub turned out to be a long, single room with a low ceiling and exposed beams. It was cluttered with round tables and ladderback chairs, and a curiously noiseless slot machine that flashed optimistically beside the door. Piled logs burned noisily in a large open fireplace at one end of the room.

The bar facing the doorway was long and highly polished, with barely a blemish to spoil its shine. Three people, a man and two women, were watching him expectantly from behind it. They were the room's sole inhabitants.

Edwards tried to contain his surprise as he crossed the thick crimson carpet and nodded a cautious greeting. The man — old Albert, unless Edwards missed his guess — was short and underweight, with straight, dark hair combed back from a broad, sloping forehead. Long, fuzzy sideburns, black shot through with grey, spread like mossy triangles across his hollow cheeks.

'Help you?' he asked.

'I hope so. I was looking for a place to stay the night. I bumped into a policeman just up the road — quite literally, in fact — and he said I should come here.'

'That'll be Old Ted,' said the landlord, exposing overlarge yellow teeth in a broad smile. 'Well, we got a room, right enough, and you're welcome to it. In fact, you're just in time. We was just about to close up.'

Close up? Edwards glanced at the clock above the fireplace, its large face yellowed by the passage of years. It was barely six o'clock: the evening was only just beginning.

'Not often we have comp'ny,' the landlord continued, offering his right hand. 'The name's Albert Small. This is the wife, Bella, and me daughter, Joyce.'

'Pleased to meet you,' said Edwards, introducing himself.

'Come far?' asked Bella. She looked cuddly and pleasant, with a round face and strong, iron-grey hair that fell to her chubby shoulders. She, like Albert, was somewhere in her late fifties. Their daughter, whose pale, almost triangular face was framed by straight blonde hair that looked fine and flyaway, studied Edwards shyly through wide blue eyes with lazy lids. She was perhaps twenty.

'London,' he replied, smiling at her.

The Smalls looked impressed. 'Well, don't just stand there, girl,' Albert said to his daughter. 'Go get the room ready while I get this gentleman a drink. What'll it be, Mr Edwards?'

'A small Scotch.'

'Scotch it is.'

Bella cleared her throat. 'Will you be wantin' a meal, Mr Edwards?'

'A snack'll do.'

'You sure? Can't beat a good hot meal after a long journey, and it's no bother.'

'No, really. I've been feeling a bit dicky

just lately. Think I'll give my stomach a rest.'

'As you wish. Cheese an' biscuits do you?'

'Lovely.'

She left them, and as Edwards sipped his whisky, Albert came around the bar and went to the doors, where he made short work of bolting them, top and bottom.

'How much do I owe you for the room?' asked Edwards.

Albert switched off the slot machine and ran his palms down his checked waistcoat. 'Well, it's not much of a room, but it's clean an' warm you'll find it,' he replied, returning to the bar. 'Tenner sound all right?'

'Fine. What about the food?'

'Tell you what,' said Albert. 'We'll throw your meals in, fair enough? Cheese 'n' biscuits tonight and a full English in the mornin'.'

It was such a good deal that Edwards paid him before he could change his mind.

A few minutes later Bella came back in

with the cheese and biscuits, the worn floorboards on her side of the bar creaking beneath her ponderous step. She set the plate before him, then backed away, all but giving him a curtsy. He cut a wedge of cheese and started to chew.

'What is it, then?' she asked suddenly.

'I'm sorry?'

'You said you haven't been feelin' well,' she replied. 'What is it, a cold or somethin'?'

'Oh, I don't know. A bit run-down, I think.'

'Run-down?' asked Albert.

Edwards took another drink, then smiled ruefully. 'Fed up with my job as much as anything.'

'Got to be happy in your work,' Bella opined, tucking her chins in like a contented budgerigar.

Edwards nodded toward the doors. 'You close a bit early, don't you?'

'Oh, dear me, no,' Bella replied. 'We always close at this time. No-one comes out after dark, you see. It'd be a waste of our time if we was to stay open. No, we usually close at six, clean up, then go up an' watch some telly.'

'Oh.'

'We get all our custom in the afternoons,' explained Albert. 'Tails off when it starts gettin' dark.' He gestured to Edwards' glass. 'Another one?'

'No, thanks.'

'Cuppa tea?' Suggested Bella.

He nodded.

'You can take it up to bed with you,' she said, lumbering heavily toward the door. She opened it, leaned on the frame and called out, 'Joyce! Put the kettle on, there's a love!' Then she came back and rested her considerable chest on the counter. 'Good girl, our Joyce. Smashing little worker. You married, are you, Mr Edwards?'

He shook his head. 'Not any more.'

'Oh,' said Bella. 'I suppose she led you a dog's life, did she?'

He wanted to tell her it was none of her business, but he didn't want to offend her, so he just said, 'Yeah,' and left it at that.

But nothing could have been further from the truth. It had all been his fault, why things hadn't worked out. He'd stay out till all hours of the night and then come in looking like death warmed over. It wasn't drink or drugs or another woman or anything like that, but Carol wouldn't believe him, so they'd split up, and Edwards had regretted it ever since.

Well, that part about the other woman wasn't strictly true. There had been a girl, just the once, about fourteen months earlier. He'd gone somewhere for the company, had a night away. He must've been blind drunk, because he hadn't been able to remember a bloody thing about it afterwards.

Anyway, they'd split up. Two months later Carol found someone else, so they divorced. She was remarried now, and had just had a baby girl by the other bloke. If things had worked out differently, the kid could have been his.

Abruptly he said, 'I think I *will* have another drink.'

'It'll mix with your tea, pet,' said Bella.

'That's all right.'

'I'm only thinking of your tummy, is all.'

'I'll risk it.'

With a shrug, Albert turned back to the optics just as Joyce came through the door, holding a cup of tea carefully in both hands. She was concentrating so hard on not spilling any that her tongue was pushing at her top lip. She put it on the bar, next to the glass.

'Thank you,' he said.

She blushed and hurried away, a nervous, slope-shouldered little mouse of a girl. Bella watched her go, a fond smile wrinkling the skin around her eyes. 'Now, you finish that Scotch,' she told Edwards, 'an' you can take your tea up to bed with you.'

A few minutes later she led him through the door behind the bar and up a narrow flight of stairs. Pictures lined the walls, flamenco dancers and little boys crying, the sort of prints that had been all the rage forty years earlier.

They reached a dimly-lit landing and Bella pointed toward a shadowy door at its far end. 'That's our rooms,' she whispered.

They climbed another flight of stairs then, to another hallway, another door. 'This is your room,' she said, and took him inside.

It was small, but as Albert had promised, it was clean and filled with the heat of a small open fire. The curtains were drawn and the sheets on the bed had been turned back. A bedside lamp cast a cosy glow up across the delicate floral wallpaper.

When she left him alone, he sat on the

edge of the bed and looked at his cup of tea. He wasn't sure he fancied it now. The fire seemed to be throwing out too much heat, but maybe that was just the fever working on him. He wasn't too worried about it. He'd felt like this before, and it always passed, eventually. Still, he didn't want to be ill in a strange place if he could help it.

He looked at his watch, then swore. It was only ten to seven. Still, maybe an early night would do him good. God knew, there'd been enough late ones in the past.

He kicked off his shoes and loosened his tie. His face was burning, and every time he moved he thought he might be sick. His tie slid snake-like through his suddenly-weak fingers and curled up on the floor. Slowly, carefully, he lay back on the bed.

His head sank into the thick pillow, and the coolness of the cotton sheets felt good against his blotchy skin. The nausea passed, but the heat and dizziness remained. *Sleep*, he told himself vaguely. *Go to sleep, and you'll feel better in the morning . . .*

When he opened his eyes again, the first thing he became aware of was the cold.

He lay there for a moment, memory coming back to him in stages. His mouth felt dry. When he tried to swallow, the effort scratched his throat and he started to cough. The fire had burned down to a mass of glowing embers. His headache was gone but he still felt rough. He reached out for the tea. It was cold and congealed, but he was so thirsty . . .

He got the cup halfway to his lips before he dropped it. The cup didn't smash, but the tea was quickly sucked right into the worn carpet. He groaned and lay back. His hands were trembling.

He shivered. His back ached and pain shot up along his spine in a series of tiny, electric shocks. *It must be the flu*, he thought groggily. Outside, he heard thunder rumble in the distance, and then the first few drops of rain began to drum gently at the window.

With an effort he got to his feet. He balanced on one leg while he tried to slip into his shoes. When he almost fell over he decided to leave them where they were and go barefoot to the bathroom and get a drink. Maybe an aspirin as well.

But then he paused. Where had Bella said the bathroom was, anyway? The silly cow, she hadn't even mentioned it.

It's probably downstairs. Bugger it: I'll just have to nose around.

He left the room quietly and, holding onto the wall to steady himself, started down the hallway to the stairs. More thunder crashed, directly overhead now, and he thought he heard the wind pick up and begin to scream.

Standing at the head of the stairs, he was suddenly reminded of just how steep and narrow they were. He wasn't sure he could negotiate them in his present state, but his throat was so *dry* . . .

Almost before he realised it, he was halfway down, arms braced weakly against the walls, body bent so that if he should lose his balance now he would fall backwards and not straight down.

When he reached the bottom step he was as weak as a kitten and sweating like a pig. He thought he was going to be sick but nothing came up. *A drink*, he told himself over and over again. *A drink, that's all I need, then I can go back to sleep. A drink and an aspirin*.

He staggered across to the door at the end of the first floor hallway. *That's our rooms*, she'd said. Lightning flickered suddenly, throwing long shadows across the floor.

He tried to knock, but his knuckles barely scraped the wood. He tried again, knocking three times, then waited. Nothing. He knocked again, one, two, three, four. No answer. He tried the door handle. It turned, but he couldn't open the door. *Locked*, he realised dimly.

Downstairs, he told himself sluggishly. *In the bar. They must have toilets down there*. He could get a drink of water, wash his face.

But it meant more stairs. He sighed. More stairs. Still, he'd already managed one lot. Bracing himself against both walls, he began his second descent.

When he was close to the bottom he sat down for a moment, panting. His hair was damp with sweat and his gums ached. He ached all over, come to think of it. *This is definitely the flu*. He forced himself back to his feet, reached for the door that led into the bar-room and pulled it open.

The first thing he heard was thunder. No, not thunder, but something that sounded very much *like* it. Hammering. A pounding that came from the far side of the room. He dismissed it, shambling into the room and working his way slowly around the bar, holding onto it and trying to focus his eyes to see where the toilets were.

The clock on the wall struck ten, and he saw them then, Albert and Bella, standing by the cellar door at the far end of the darkened room. They turned and looked at him, fear and guilt carved into their bloodless faces.

The pounding that came from the other side of the door was louder than ever now, the screaming of the wind not the wind at all, but screaming nonetheless: a wailing that also came from the other side of the door.

He stood watching them for what seemed like a long time, frowning. They just stared back at him, unmoving. Then Albert stepped forward, nodding nervously to him. Edwards tried to speak but his throat was so dry he couldn't make the right sounds.

'You're here at last, then,' said Albert.

Behind him, Bella pressed her face against the door and called through it, 'Be quiet, Joyce, be quiet! He's here now!'

Immediately, the pounding and whining died away, and the warm air was filled only with the rattle of the falling rain outside, the spit and snap of logs burning in the hearth, and Edwards' heavy, tortured breathing. He tried to speak again, but then gave up with a shake of his head.

Albert said, 'We knew you'd come back. Oh, it took time, 'course it did. But we knew you'd come back eventually.'

Bella came forward to join him,

wringing her meaty hands together nervously. 'Been breaking her heart, it has,' she said, nodding to the cellar door. 'The loneliness. Being one of a kind. Some nights it's been terrible. But I told her it wouldn't always be like that. I said you'd come back to her one day. And you have.'

He wondered what they were going on about, but then his attention was taken by something else. The dizziness was wearing off. He could feel the strength flooding back into his limbs. The pain in his spine was receding and he was able to breathe easier.

He watched as Bella went back to the cellar door and said through it, 'Now, you be a good girl, Joyce, an' don't do anythin' foolish. I'm goin' to open the door now.'

She unbolted the door, top and bottom, then turned a key in the lock. She paused, looking carefully into her husband's face. When he nodded, she turned the handle and pulled the door open.

Edwards wasn't sure what he expected

to see. He could just about make out the first few steps that led down into the cellar, but everything else was lost in black shadow. He heard someone shuffling about in the darkness, sniffing and whining.

It was only when Joyce finally came up out of the cellar that he remembered everything — everything he had forgotten.

'She needed a mate,' said Albert, almost apologetically. 'That's why we let her bite you, last time you stayed.'

'Must be about fourteen month ago, now,' added Bella. 'Took a fair while for your instincts to come out, but they did. Eventually. They led you back here. To *her*.'

He narrowed his eyes. He *remembered* them! He *did* remember them! And looking once, briefly, into the mirror behind the bar, he saw what he had become, and knew then that it hadn't been the flu or anything like it, but rather, the *Change*. He would get used to it in time. With every full moon it would become easier.

'She needed a mate,' Albert repeated, and watched as Edwards padded across to Joyce, licked and sniffed at her, and then led her back down into the cellar, wagging his tail expectantly.

Beware of the House

We were driving along one of those narrow, slightly claustrophobic lanes you find in the country, just out for a drive and discovering new places, when Lynn suddenly said, 'Alan, stop the car a minute! Did you see that sign?'

'What sign?' I asked.

'Back there, on the right.'

I pulled over and we sat there for a moment, the only sounds the low purring of the car engine and the pleasant chirp and chatter of birds in the nearby hedgerow.

It was a blinding August Sunday, and the temperature was well up in the eighties. We'd woken early that morning and decided on impulse to get out of town for the day, and according to the map we weren't far from a village called Maplewick now, where we were hoping to find a country pub at which to spend a lazy afternoon.

'All right,' I said. 'I give in. What's so special about a sign, then?'

I often ribbed Lynn about her curiosity. I could never understand why she took such a great interest in everything the neighbours did: where they went, who they went with, what time they left, what time they came back. But this thing about signs was a new one on me.

'I think I saw what it said, but I must've been mistaken,' she replied, as if that made it all perfectly clear.

'Oh.'

'It's just back there, by that five-bar gate,' she added meaningfully.

I couldn't really see the point in going all the way back just to read a sign, but it was a glorious day and I was in too good a mood to argue, so I reversed back up the lane until we came to the gate.

'I *thought* that's what it said,' muttered Lynn.

I could see it myself, now. It was a large sheet of weather-warped ply nailed crookedly to a post, the words daubed in red against a grubby white background. It said:

PLEASE DO NOT GO BEYOND THIS POINT OWING TO THE REPUTATION OF THE HOUSE

Our eyes turned from the sign to the gate, about forty metres beyond which a large, red-brick house thrust up from a sea of waist-high yellow grass.

It was an odd, lop-sided sort of place. There was no sense of balance to it at all. A fat, round tower with a pointed roof which had long-since caved in projected crookedly from the left-side front corner. At ground level a covered porch that was painted the same dull burgundy as the peeling window frames wrapped itself possessively around the property's right side.

To my eye, the house was all jarring lines and angles — *asymmetrical* was the polite word for it — and it seemed to owe its design to a hotch-potch of clashing architectural styles, everything from Georgian to Bauhaus, with a touch of Gothic, Jacobean and even what I took to be Deconstructivism thrown in for bad measure.

Spiky, misshapen weeds sprang from cracks in the walls, and black holes gaped in the steep roof, where hefty grey slates had slipped and fallen over the years. Tall chimneys stabbed at the sky like accusing fingers, and the remains of a filthy, water-stained *fleur de lis*-style gingerbread fascia clung to the front elevation as if for dear life.

The tall, thin sash windows at ground level had been boarded up, and those upstairs that hadn't been smashed by vandals, plus two porthole windows in the gables that looked unsettlingly like a pair of eyes, just about managed to reflect the clear blue sky through thick layers of dirt.

Seeing fluorescent silver graffiti staining the lower walls in a series of broad, mad squiggles, I shook my head. In its way it had probably been an impressive place once — well, *unique*, certainly — but now it was just old and humiliated.

'What do you suppose it means?' asked Lynn, returning her attention to the sign.

I shrugged. 'It means please do not go beyond this point owing to the rep — '

'Very funny,' she cut in. 'But *really*,

Alan. What do you suppose it means, 'the reputation of the house'?'

In my mind I could see a colourful salad being washed down by something long and cool. I was hungry and thirsty and didn't want to think about signs that didn't make any sense. 'I don't know. Maybe it's unsafe,' I offered. 'It looks like it's about ready to fall down.'

Lynn climbed out of the car and slowly walked over to the post, her freckled face tilted up to read the sign again. A moment later she began to fumble with the latch on the gate, and I got out of the car quickly.

'Whoa, there! Where do you think *you're* going?'

She threw me a mischievous smile. She was in her middle thirties now, but when she smiled like that I thought I knew what she must have been like when she was a kid. 'Exploring,' she said.

'Oh, come on — '

'Well, you've got to admit, it *is* a mystery.'

'Not at all,' I replied. 'And even if it was, we're not the Famous Five. Come on, forget it. It's none of our business. Let's try and find that pub.'

Ignoring me, Lynn said, 'It's no good, the latch is rusted. We'll have to climb over.'

'Lynn, this is private property!'

'But — '

'Hello there! Need some help?'

We both turned quickly, stupidly trying not to look too guilty. Striding towards us from down the lane was a stocky, big-bellied man in his late sixties, with shaggy white hair protruding from beneath his ancient fedora hat. His face was red from the sun and a lifetime of clean country air, his shirt-sleeves were rolled up and his mustard-coloured waistcoat was unbuttoned. In his left hand he held a dog-lead, which he tapped against his leg as he approached us. The dog to whom it belonged, a sleek black collie-cross, padded along at his heels, its long pink tongue drooping tiredly from one side of his mouth. Hot as he was, however, the animal still managed a half-hearted wag of the tail in greeting.

'Lost, are you?' asked the man.

I was just about to say yes, when Lynn said, 'Actually, we were just wondering about this sign.'

Blabbermouth, I thought.

'Oh?' said the man. The dog sat down and I bent to scratch one of his ears so that I would be spared some of the embarrassment Lynn was causing me. The man said, 'What about it?'

'We were wondering about the wording.'

The man glanced at the property beyond the gate. 'It refers to Midnight House,' he said.

'That's the name of this place, is it?'

'Aye.'

When she realised he wasn't going to volunteer any more information, Lynn said, 'It's just that we thought it was a bit odd. I mean, why not just say 'Trespassers will be prosecuted' or something?'

The man studied her carefully, and threw me a somewhat briefer examination as I straightened back up. Quietly, he said, 'Becuz . . . Listen, mum. Midnight House isn't like your usual, everyday vacant property. It . . . well, it's *different*.'

'What do you mean?' I asked, surprised at the sound of my own voice.

He shifted to a more comfortable position. 'Well, you can call me a liar or a leg-puller,' he said, and I got the feeling he used this line at the beginning of every tall story he told, 'but Midnight House is what you'd call *haunted*.'

'What?' asked Lynn, her mouth dropping open. 'I mean, *why*?'

He shrugged. 'Who knows? The house has stood there nigh on two hundred years, and in all that time there's not been one owner who's been happy with it. I dunno, it's like there's something *bad* about it that attracts misery and ill-fortune. 'Course, you could just write it off to coincidence, but it certainly does seem as if one tragedy after another has befallen the owners of Midnight House. And not just the owners, neither. They say it's got polter-whatsits an' everythin'.'

'Poltergeists,' supplied Lynn.

'Them as well,' the man nodded. 'There're two reasons to steer clear of Midnight House. One — it's evil. I don't know why, it just *is*.' He leaned on the gate and stared at the place, whether for effect or not I couldn't tell.

'And two?' I asked.

He turned his warm blue eyes on me. 'Midnight House hates people,' he replied quietly. 'It just *hates* 'em.'

I know it was only my imagination, but suddenly the day seemed to cool right off, and the air grew so still and quiet that I could hear insects buzzing in the cool shadows on the far side of the lane. Lynn must have felt the atmosphere change too, because she took my arm and gave the nervous little giggle she usually reserved for late-night horror films.

'You think I'm havin' you on,' the man observed without criticism. 'I'm not. Here, I'll show you.' He looked up, squinting at the sky. Then, 'See them geese up there?'

We looked up and saw some birds flapping across the sky in a wide V formation, honking as they went.

'Watch when they fly near the house,' he told us.

As we watched, it seemed that they made a wide sweep that took them *around* the property rather than directly over it. We noticed other birds, too, crows, kingfishers, skylarks and starlings: none of them would fly *over* the house or the once-landscaped grounds in which it stood, but always skirted around it instead.

'See?' the man asked, but there was no smugness in his tone. 'The birds know there's somethin' evil there. An' not just the birds. *Jack!*'

The collie-cross pricked up his ears, watching with loyal brown eyes as his master picked up a thin branch that had fallen by the hedge. Stripping it of its leaves, he made ready to throw it. 'Fetch, boy!'

The dog was a blur as he took off up the lane after the stick, his weariness of a moment before now forgotten. His bushy tail wagged triumphantly as he brought it back and dropped it at his master's feet. As he looked up, waiting for praise, it seemed for all the world as if he were smiling.

The man picked the stick up and threw it over the gate and into the field.

'Fetch, Jack!'

But instead of leaping up and over the gate, the dog sat down and gave an apologetic whine. His head bowed, his ears dropped and when he looked up, two white half-moons showed beneath his eyes.

'All right, boy, all right.'

The man bent and fixed the lead to the dog's collar. Straightening up again, he tried to drag the animal nearer the gate. Stubbornly the dog dug his paws into the ground and stiffened his legs defiantly. His hackles went up, and to our surprise a low, deep growl issued from deep inside him.

Then the man was bending again, unhooking the lead and rubbing the dog's head vigorously. 'All right, boy, all right,' he said, adding, 'Never disobeyed me before, this dog. But he'd sooner go for me than go anywhere near *that* place.'

As he stroked the dog's head, the fur along its back settled down, and as if to reaffirm their relationship, the animal licked his hand several times before he stood up again.

'After that last trouble, we had psychics and all sorts down here, prodding and poking about with machines and meters and such. 'Course, all their equipment couldn't tell 'em a thing. Midnight House is too clever to give its secrets away.'

'The last trouble?' asked Lynn.

He nodded. 'Young Todd Lampton an' a couple of his mates slipped out of school early one afternoon a couple of months back and came down here to paint the walls with their blummin' giraffity.'

'Graffiti?' I said.

'Aye, that's the animal,' he replied. 'Blummin' vandals.'

So that's where the fluorescent silver shapes and squiggles had come from. 'What happened?' I asked.

He shrugged. 'Don't suppose anyone knows for sure. But there they were, havin' a high old time, when all of a sudden it clouded up an' started to rain. Todd was all for breakin' into the house, but his mates wouldn't hear of it. They ran off to find shelter elsewhere, an' left him to it.'

'Well, Todd called 'em fourteen different kinds of coward, then forced his way inside, out of the rain, more to prove a point than anythin' else, I 'spect.'

'And what happened?' I asked again.

'Don't know,' came the reply. 'No-one ever saw Todd Lampton again.'

'Christ,' I muttered.

'Christ doesn't come into it,' he said. 'Anyway, we thought it was high time we put a sign up. That place is best left alone, and folks've got a right to be warned about it.' He studied it for another thoughtful moment through narrowed, far-away eyes. 'Only things that thrive there are the weeds,' he muttered. Then he brightened a little. 'Well, I'd better be on my way. The wife'll be wonderin' where I've got to.' He looked at both of us in turn. 'Take care, you two. An' leave well enough alone.'

He turned back once to give us a wave, and then he and his dog disappeared around a bend and we were left alone once more.

'Come on, then,' I said, turning to get back into the car.

But Lynn held onto my arm, and when I turned back to her, she gave it a squeeze.

'Now what?' I asked a little irritably.

'Shall we take a closer look?' she suggested.

I could hardly believe my ears. 'After what that old bloke just said? You're joking!'

'Oh, come on, Alan. Where's your sense of adventure?'

'Funnily enough,' I replied, 'I left it back home. Right next to my willingness to trespass.'

'Oh, Alan — '

'No.'

'*Please?*'

I took another look at the house, wondering if there *would* be any harm in it. It was broad daylight, after all, and by now the goose bumps on my arms had gone down. I let my breath out in a loud sigh.

'All right. But only because I don't want you sulking for the rest of the afternoon.'

She smiled sweetly. 'Come on, then.'

'After you. Ladies before gentlemen and all that.'

'What happened to age before beauty?'

Well, I couldn't argue with that, so we climbed over the gate together, leaving the safe normality of the lane behind, and immediately we were struck by the absolute silence that met us.

No insects buzzed or fluttered in that field. No breeze dared to disturb its near-photographic stillness. The temperature seemed to have dropped several degrees, and once or twice I'm sure I saw my breath coming in wintry clouds.

We glanced at each other, then began to walk toward the house, following the wide, weed-choked curve of what once must have been a sweeping gravel drive. What was left of the gravel crunched softly beneath our feet, and even though I knew we were all alone, I couldn't shake the feeling that we were being watched.

Overhead, a large black crow flew around us.

'Did you know that a flock of crows is called a murder?' asked Lynn, more to break the silence than anything else.

'No, I didn't.'

'Well, it is.'

I glanced back over one shoulder. We seemed to have covered an awful lot of ground in a very short space of time. When I returned my attention to the house, I thought I saw movement: little white flashes in a dozen different places, which appeared for just an instant before shooting up or down or off to one side and disappearing.

Was that my imagination, too? I didn't know what to think, but I hoped it was my eyes playing tricks on me.

We must have been mad to enter this place, I thought. But enter it we had, so we might as well get a closer look at the infamous Midnight House while we were here. At least it would be a story we could dine out on in time to come.

The house stared back at us through its grime-blinded windows, silver graffiti clinging to its red-brick walls like tinsel on a dead Christmas tree, and if houses have character, then this one's *was* evil, just as the old man had said.

We lifted our arms high as we began to

wade through the tall, dead grass, and in the same moment that a shadow skittered across the ground about ten metres ahead of us, something in the air caught my eye. I thought at first that it was a bird, that a bird was actually flying *across* the field instead of around it.

But no bird was that shape.

It was a moment before I realised that it was going to land where we had stopped to watch it, and clumsily I grabbed Lynn's arm and yanked her roughly to one side just as the long grass shuddered and rippled with the impact of its landing.

The grass whispered dryly as it swayed back and forth.

Gingerly, we leaned forward to see what had struck the earth, and my mouth turned dry when I saw that it was a brick.

A red brick.

The same kind of brick from which Midnight House was built.

Someone was in their somewhere, a squatter, perhaps, or maybe even this so-called 'missing' boy, Todd Lampton, and he was trying to scare us off.

But then a sound reached our ears in that otherwise silent field like a cork popping from a bottle, and we saw another brick arcing toward us, twisting end over end through the air.

I might have been mistaken, but as near as I could tell, it seemed to have pushed itself out of the wall facing us.

It was then that I realised with a sudden flash of insight that the house *itself* was attacking us.

Swearing, I grabbed Lynn's wrist and we began to run back toward the gate. Behind us we heard the brick crash heavily into the grass.

Another popping sound came then, but we didn't have to look back to know that it was another brick, or worse still a sharp-edged slate from the roof that would shear off a hand or a foot if it were to catch you at just the right angle.

Stones flew up beneath our heels as we continued to race along the gravel drive, but no matter how fast we ran, the gate ahead never seemed to get any closer. To make matters worse, it suddenly dawned on me that the weeds themselves were snatching at us, and anything that could slow us down with hooks, prickles or thorns appeared to be doing so.

Lynn stumbled and for one dreadful moment I thought she was going to fall, but then she righted herself again and on we ran. I could hear the rasping of her breath and felt my own head spinning madly with the same repeated thought.

It's attacking us, it's really attacking us, the house is attacking us . . .

Then we reached the gate and threw ourselves over it and back into the lane. Our faces were flushed and glistening, our shoulders heaving as we sucked greedily at the warm air. We didn't talk. We didn't have the energy for that. We just exchanged one brief, deep, serious look, and then we got into the car and drove quickly away from that place where evil lived.

We didn't stop driving for a very long time.

We've never told anyone about what happened to us on that bright August Sunday. Who'd believe us, except the people of Maplewick, who put the sign there in the first place?

Still, it's all down on paper now, and Lynn and I both agree that as bizarre as it was, what we experienced that afternoon has made us appreciate all that is good just that *little* bit more. I know it sounds corny, but it's just the way we feel.

As the old man told us, there's something wrong with Midnight House. It *does* seem to hate people, and if such a thing is possible, then I believe it also really *does* attract evil, though *why* is anyone's guess.

Anyway, we were lucky. Others might *not* be.

So, if you should ever find yourself near Maplewick, and happen to see that sign by the gate, please, *please* heed its warning.

Take some advice of two people who very nearly found out the hard way . . . and Beware of the House.

Shadow of Doubt

You couldn't blame us for being overprotective of Daniel. We'd come so close to losing him in those first few weeks of his life that Alex and I swore that we'd never, *ever* take him for granted.

We'd spent months trying to prepare ourselves for the worst, of course. Well, when your forty-two year-old wife announces that she's pregnant — and for the first time — you suddenly become disturbingly aware of all the things which can, and so often *do*, go wrong.

Sure enough, when Daniel was born he was six weeks premature and weighed just over four pounds.

Even now, thinking back to what he looked like trapped inside his incubator, catching every tic and twitch of his wrinkled face and flex of his tiny red hands, I remember trying not to love him, and knowing that if I did, the pain of losing him — as I was sure we *must*

— would crush me.

I couldn't stop myself, though. Well, he was my son. My *son*.

As the days grew into a week, a fortnight and then three weeks, he grew stronger. And if there really was a God in Heaven, then He certainly did answer our prayers.

It was only after he started school that I began to realise just how *young* the parents of all his friends were. I was fifty and here I was with a seven year-old son. Somehow, even in this day and age, it didn't feel quite right, and I sometimes wondered if Daniel felt uncomfortable about it as well. His father was old enough to be his *grand*father.

If it bothered him, however, he never showed it. He was always here and there, into everything, a happy, funny, mischievous bundle of energy. He was such a live wire that sometimes it was all I could do to keep up with him.

But then . . .

Then . . .

It began one chilly September Saturday, and I had just come back from getting the papers. Autumn was in the air, and the smell of it reminded me of dead leaves and Christmas. When I got back to the house, Alex was dishing up breakfast, and Daniel was sitting at the table, staring into his bowl of Coco Pops. I threw the papers on the table and sat down across from him.

'Morning, Tiger,' I said.

He made no reply.

I leaned across the table and touched his small arm. 'Come on,' I said. 'Wakey, wakey.'

He looked up then, and his eyes were not the eyes of a young, healthy boy, but those of an old, old man — watery, faintly bloodshot and dreadfully, dreadfully sad.

'Morning,' he mumbled.

'You all right, Dan?' I asked.

He nodded, as if he couldn't summon

the energy to reply any other way.

'What's up?'

'He's tired,' said Alex, coming over to the table. She was tall and just a little heavy, and her oval face was framed by long auburn hair. As I looked up at her, I saw for the first time just how much older she'd started looking, and it wasn't so much a revelation as a shock.

I looked at him again. 'Couldn't you sleep, Dan?'

'No.'

'Bad dreams?'

He looked at me again, and his expression made me feel cold. 'No.'

'Do you — '

'Can I go back to bed?' he asked.

Alex ran a hand through his corn-yellow hair and then took hold of his hand. ''Course you can,' she said. 'Come on, Tiger.'

But he slipped his hand out of hers and slid off the chair. 'It's all right,' he muttered. 'I can go by myself.'

That was typical Daniel, of course. He'd always hated any kind of fuss. We watched him leave the room, our own breakfasts forgotten.

'What's wrong with him?' I asked softly.

Alex shrugged. 'Maybe he's got a cold working on him.'

I nodded. 'I'll go and read him a story or something.'

But when I went up to his room, Daniel was sound asleep.

He slept for most of that day, his little chest rising and falling slowly beneath the cover I'd put over him. Watching from his bedroom doorway, I saw his delicate hands clench and unclench, saw the film of sweat rise on his brow, but when I reached down to lay the back of my hand across his forehead, he didn't seem to be feverish. He was actually chilled.

I'd always secretly dreaded the responsibility of having children. When the doctor had first told Alex she was pregnant, I'd received the news with mixed emotions. Up until then my life had been orderly and predictable, and that's the way I liked it. In some respects, I felt almost resentful that something would happen in nine months' time — well, seven and a half, as it turned out — that would change my precious routine forever.

Much as I liked the idea of being a

father, I dreaded having to be responsible for another human being. I was the same when I was a boy myself and it came to pets. I remember feeling so helpless when my first goldfish died, when our dog Sassy got too old and feeble to go out into the garden. Helpless. I couldn't work a miracle and restore them to health: and in the same way, all I could do now was watch Daniel sleeping the day away, and pray that when he woke up, he'd feel better.

But he didn't.

When he finally got up he looked even more exhausted than he had before he went back to bed. His eyes were dark-ringed and sunken, his skin the colour of turnips. And at bedtime, after an evening spent watching TV without noticeable enthusiasm, he tried to put off going to bed.

'I want to stay up with you,' he argued in an uncharacteristic whine.

I looked at him, into those eyes as blue-green as my own, and saw with surprise that he was close to tears. He really was dreading having to go to bed. He was a tough little fellow, my Daniel, tough and self-reliant, and at the same time as sensitive and kind-hearted as Alex. He would grow up to be a very fine man, I thought. But right now . . .

'You know the rules,' I said.

'But I'm not tired. I — '

'Dan,' I said, and tried to put a firm

edge into my otherwise gentle tone, 'it's time for bed. Come on now, no arguments.'

He wanted to say something more but stopped, then turned and looked at Alex. She reached out and took his hand. 'Come on,' she said, getting up. 'Let's get you all washed and ready.'

I kissed him goodnight and watched Alex lead him upstairs to the bathroom.

Every time I looked in on him that night, I found him wide awake and watching the doorway, the duvet bunched up around his tiny body like restless waves on a frozen sea. Around us, the house was dark and near-silent. The only movement came from the boat mobile hanging from the ceiling, a wooden lighthouse surrounded by lifebuoys and brightly-coloured wooden yachts, stirred by the softest, slightest breeze. In the glow of his Lily the Elephant night-light I saw his pale face and impossibly big, liquid eyes, watching me.

'Still can't sleep, Tiger?' I asked.

He didn't reply immediately. Then, his voice sounding sad and lonely, he said, 'No.'

'Bad dreams again?'

He didn't reply at all.

On Sunday morning he looked even worse. He said he didn't feel ill, and he didn't have a temperature, but he looked absolutely shattered. He didn't want to go out, he didn't want to *play* out. The only thing he could bring himself to do was sit in the living room with his hands clasped in his lap, and when he tired of that, he slouched outside, sat on the stairs for a while, then at the window, just watching, waiting. He hardly said a word and couldn't bring himself to eat anything at all.

By Sunday evening, after we'd had to force him to go to bed again, Alex decided to take him to see the doctor, and I had to admit, the sooner we tackled whatever was ailing him, the better.

Alex took him to see Dr Sheikh the following morning. He was a tall man with kind, rounded features and an excellent bedside manner. He examined Daniel and then asked him exactly how he felt. Daniel was always wary around people he saw only rarely, but did as he was told.

Alex told me all about it when I phoned home that afternoon. 'He's having nightmares,' she said, lowering her voice so that Daniel, who was sitting in front of the TV, wouldn't hear.

'What did I tell you?' I said.

'Yeah, yeah, you know best,' she replied. 'Still, when you asked him, he said he wasn't.'

'Well, you know kids. What happened, anyway?'

'The doctor says it's common between the ages of one to ten years and that he'll grow out of it.'

'That's that, then.'

'Yes,' she agreed. 'But he's still not eating. The doctor said not to worry about that, either. He'll eat when he's hungry. But he hasn't eaten anything since Friday night. I mean, he's a growing boy — '

'That's the point,' I hurried to assure her. 'He's a growing boy, and right now he's going through a phase.'

'Oh, Mike — '

'A *phase*,' I repeated. 'We've all had them.'

'He's a bit young for puberty.'

'I'm not talking about puberty,' I said, vaguely uncomfortable with the thought. 'Look, this time tomorrow he'll be back to normal and it'll be all Top Trumps and Racing Grannies again.'

'I do hope so.'

'Don't worry. It'll all be all right.'

I was just about to hang up when something else occurred to me. 'What's he been dreaming about, anyway? Did he say?'

'Well, that's the funny thing,' said Alex. 'At his age, it should be all Top Trumps and Racing Grannies, like you said.'

'But . . . ?'

'But he's dreaming about *vampires*,' she said softly.

By Tuesday evening Daniel still wasn't showing any improvement. Now, as I looked at him, lying there in his bed, surrounded by toys and mobiles and all the happy things of childhood, I could see that he'd lost weight and his hair seemed flat and dull. His eyes were flat as well, flat and somehow . . . resigned. It was as if he were just waiting for death, and I had to remind myself that he was just seven years old. My son was just seven.

I sat beside him and reached down to stroke his face. 'How are you feeling, Tiger?' I asked.

He shrugged. 'Okay.'

God, I thought, *what a child*. Even in this sorry state he wasn't one to grumble. But why did being so lucky make me want to weep?

'Still having dreams?' I asked.

He looked up at the ceiling, declining to answer.

'Is there anything you want to tell me?'

'No.'

'You sure?'

He looked at me then. 'Yes.'

I reached down and took hold of his hands. They were like ice. 'Tell me about these . . . dreams, Dan.'

I saw his eyes widen a little with dread.

'Come on, I want to know all about them. Then we can fight them off together.'

I could see that he was thinking it over. 'Come on, Dan,' I said gently. 'Tell me.'

He mumbled something, but it was so soft I couldn't make it out. 'What was that?' I asked.

'Every night,' he muttered.

'Yes,' I prompted.

His eyes went to the doorway behind me. 'Someone,' he said, 'stands there.'

I threw a glance over my shoulder, then turned back to face him. The smile I gave him was meant to reassure, but I couldn't hold it in place for very long. 'Someone?' I repeated.

He shook his head slowly, as if the

effort hurt him. 'Some*thing*,' he corrected himself. His breath came harshly now. 'Yellow eyes,' he whispered. 'And hairy. I told the doctor.'

'Sure you did. But tell *me*.'

He kept his eyes on the bedroom door. 'Yellow eyes,' he said again. 'And there's the teeth, as well. Fangs.'

I squeezed his hand tighter, but I doubt that he was even aware of my presence just then. 'All right,' I said softly. 'Dad's here.'

His eyes came back to me then.

'Do you want anything to eat?'

'No.'

'Drink?'

'No.'

'Is there *anything* I can get you?'

He wanted to speak to me again, I could tell by his eyes. There was something he wanted to say, but then the light in them died and he shook his head. 'No.'

I swallowed and bent to kiss his cheek. All at once the urge to weep stronger than ever. When I stood up, he let go of my hand reluctantly.

'Go to sleep,' I managed.

'I'll try.'

'You won't dream,' I predicted, trying to sound convincing.

'I *don't* dream,' he replied coldly.

When I went back downstairs, Alex took one look at my face and said, 'It's serious, isn't it? More serious than we thought, I mean.'

I flopped down onto the sofa. 'I don't know. Yes. I suppose it is. He's not ill — '

'Not physically.'

'No, not physically. But . . . ' I shrugged. 'It's like he's taken these nightmares and blown them out of all proportion.'

'Sure. But it's not right, Mike. A boy of that age, dreaming about vampires.'

'Hardly vampires,' I said.

'What?'

'Oh, nothing. It's not important.'

'Well, we've got to do *something*,' she said.

I looked at her, not sure how to say what I had to say next. 'Do you think we should take him to see a psychiatrist?'

I really didn't know how she was going to take it. She looked at me for a very long time. And then she said, 'I've already found one.'

Her name was Dr Helen Usha, B.A., MSc, D.Psych, and she wasn't a psychiatrist, she was a child psychologist. She operated from a very exclusive address in West London. I took a day off work and Alex and I took Daniel to see her two days later.

Dr Usha turned out to be a short black woman with harshly cropped grey hair. She did everything slowly. She greeted us slowly. She showed us to chairs slowly, she took her own seat behind an enormous desk slowly, and then she studied all three of us slowly. Or maybe it just seemed that way because she charged by the hour — she charged a *lot* by the hour.

'Now,' she said in a low, gentle voice. 'I understand that this is all to do with your son, Daniel, here, yes?'

I said that it was.

'And what exactly is the problem?'

‘Well, he’s been having a lot of dreams lately. Nightmares.’

‘That is not unusual in the young,’ said Dr Usha, stating the blindingly obvious.

‘But these dreams,’ I persisted, ‘they’re full of monsters, and they’re affecting his health.’

She picked up an expensive fountain pen and held it ready over a sheet of paper. ‘Has he been under any particular stresses recently?’

‘No.’

‘Does he see you and your wife argue at all?’

‘No.’

‘So there is no . . . tension, as such.’

‘No.’

‘He is a bright student?’

‘He does okay.’

‘When does he have these nightmares?’

I shrugged. ‘At night.’

‘I mean, does he have them within the first hour or two of sleep?’

I looked down at him. ‘Dan?’ I asked.

He shook his head. ‘Later.’

Dr Usha sucked air in through her nose and scribbled some notes.

‘I was wondering,’ I said. ‘Could they be night terrors?’ I’d heard the expression on TV once, or maybe I’d read about it in the paper.

‘Why do you ask?’ she countered.

‘I just . . . wondered.’

‘Did you suffer from night terrors when *you* were a child?’

‘No.’

‘Mrs Collins?’

Alex shook her head. ‘No. Nothing like that.’

‘Then I doubt it,’ Dr Usha replied. ‘Night terrors are usually hereditary. The sufferer is unable to wake from them, and remembers little if anything about them after the event. Now, from what I understand, Daniel here wakes up and *remembers* them.’

Daniel shook his head. ‘They’re not dreams,’ he said.

The doctor wrote something else down.

‘He won’t eat, and he’s afraid to go to bed at night,’ offered Alex.

‘Well, we can’t have that,’ said the doctor, turning her attention to Daniel. ‘Come and sit down for a moment,

Daniel. I want to ask you some questions.'

She interrogated him for about thirty minutes, while Alex and I sat in nervous silence, watching, listening and generally trying to pretend for Daniel's sake that we weren't really there at all. Dr Usha scribbled notes all the time, then finally sat back and offered us her most reassuring smile. Daniel went over to a table beneath the window, where he amused himself with Dr Usha's Newton's Cradle, click-click, click-click.

'Although he insists that these dreams of his are not dreams at all,' the doctor began, 'they are in fact merely fantasies which originate in the darker side of his personality. Although he *claims* to be afraid of them, he secretly finds it *exciting* to dream about monsters with fangs.'

Alex sounded as disappointed as I felt. 'But he's a seven year-old boy. A *normal* seven year-old boy. He doesn't understand anything about the darker side of life.'

'Doesn't he? Does he have access to the internet?'

'Yes.'

'*Supervised* access?'

'Not always, no.'

Dr Usha spread her hands. 'Then potentially he has access to a wealth of material from which he could easily have drawn this fantasy, much of it quite legitimately aimed at children.'

I had to admit, grudgingly, that she had a point. *Buffy the Vampire Slayer*, *Count Duckula*, *Bunnicula*, Harry Potter — they all had a lot to answer for.

'So?' I asked.

'I believe your son is having difficulty differentiating between what is real and what is imaginary, Mr Collins. This is not at all uncommon. We all suffer from it, to one degree or another, mostly when we are either very young, or very old. In that period between sleeping and waking, it is hard to decide what is real and what is not. In your son's case, he believes that the figure that visits him each night is *real*, and that is the essence of the problem.'

'What can we do about it, then?'

Dr Usha sucked up some more air. 'I

would like to see him again in two weeks' time. Next time, I will talk to him about the dreams he has had in the past, as well as the ones causing all the problems at the moment, and in that way I will convince him that they are, after all, just dreams. He has developed a phobia, but together, by talking about them, we will give him the necessary tools with which to identify and accept them for what they are.'

Alex glanced across at me, then said, 'And what can we do in the meantime?'

'Keep him occupied, get him started on a new hobby or interest. Monitor his sleep patterns and keep a diary.'

'Is that it?'

It was a moment before I recognised my own voice.

Dr Usha's smile widened. She had lovely teeth, I thought.

'That's it,' she replied. 'At least, for the moment. Unless the problem fails to resolve itself spontaneously, we can discuss drug treatment.' She glanced from me to Alex and said, 'You were perhaps expecting more?'

Alex said, 'I don't know. I suppose so. I just don't understand how these dreams of his can be so vivid.'

'But they *can*, I assure you.'

'Do you see any . . . symbolism in them?'

'Not especially. He sleeps well until he senses a shadow falling across his face. Then he wakes up, and that is when he sees what he describes as a vampire.'

'It can't be a vampire,' I said.

'Of course it can't,' she agreed.

'Vampires don't cast shadows,' I told her.

That night I lay in bed, unable, unwilling, to sleep. Beside me, Alex stirred briefly, her own sleep troubled. As tired as we all were by the time we got home, it had taken her a long time to drift off, but she'd managed it eventually and I was glad.

I was warm and thirsty and irritable, and I wanted to look in on Daniel. I got up gently so as not to wake Alex, and sat there for a moment, just thinking about this whole sorry mess.

After a while I got up and left the bedroom. The landing outside was dark, the night so quiet you could actually hear the silence hiss. But everything about the place had changed. It was no longer the warm and comfortable, child-free home I always used to look forward to coming home to. Now it held misery and despair.

I looked down at my hands. They were —

But by then I was in Daniel's room, was closing the door softly behind me, and when my shadow fell across his face he opened his eyes and looked up at me, and there was absolute terror in him.

His eyes were large, liquidy. His mouth worked but he made no sound. Above me, the little yacht mobile twisted lazily.

I stood over him, watching him, and as I did so, I felt my teeth — my *fangs* — lengthen and push my mouth open. Coarse brown hair was bristling all over my face and body now, and even as I reached for him, my fingernails were no longer fingernails, they were *claws*.

I looked down at him, at this boy whose presence I had so selfishly, jealously come to resent, and knew he was too scared to scream. He was mine for the taking now. I could take him any time I wished, so long as the moon was full.

I tried to hold myself back, as I had done for the past six nights. I tried to resist the urge to reach down and kill my son.

But finally, as I had always known it would, the urge proved too strong.

Loathe Story

Where did it all go wrong, Carla? Why does it have to end this way? We never did anyone any harm. Well, we never *meant* to. But now look at us — you folded up in the corner, all wide-eyed and scared, and me with a gun in my hand.

Carla, don't start crying again. *Please*. I've got to do it: you *know* I have. And don't try to speak. You know you can't.

Oh Christ, what a mess . . .

I was a fool to ever let it go this far. I mean, even to *think* there could've been a future for us . . .

But I let my heart rule my head, didn't I? And now we both have to pay the price.

I wouldn't mind, but all I wanted was a friend. Was that asking too much? If I'd been rich and famous or just better *company*, I could've had all the friends I wanted. But because I'm just a nobody, an ugly, tongue-tied fifty year-old who still lives with his mum and isn't much good in a crowd . . .

Carla, *please* don't cry. I've cried enough for both of us, believe me. It's going to kill me to pull this trigger on you. It'll be like dying even before I stick the barrel in my mouth and blow my own brains out.

Yes, yes, I know you love me. I love *you*, too. Perhaps if I didn't love you so much, it wouldn't have gone this far.

If only I could turn the clock back to last March, and know then what I know now. If only I'd known what would happen when Mum first asked me to come up here because the roof was leaking.

Mum and Dad hadn't come up here in years, of course. Well, you wouldn't expect them to, at their age. But I always liked coming up here and sorting through my old toys and comics. That's called *nostalgia*.

Anyway, it didn't take long to spot where the rain was coming in. One of the roof tiles around the rear chimney breast had been displaced by the wind. I pulled it back into place as best I could, but it was only a temporary job, so I left a plastic bucket beneath it just in case it should slip and start leaking again.

I was just turning to go back downstairs when I noticed something glistening on the floorboards, like the trail a snail leaves behind it, only wider: about sixteen *inches* wide. It weaved this way and that, all over the loft, and I wondered why I'd never noticed it before, but the beam of the torch had to hit it at just the right angle before it would reflect the light. If it didn't, you'd never even know it was there.

I followed it with the torchlight. It got lost in a number of similar, older trails, but I always managed to pick it up again. Bent double so my head wouldn't hit the rafters, I followed it to the farthest corner, where the shadows and the cobwebs were thickest.

And there, cowering in one of the deepest nooks and crannies, I found *you*.

What *were* you? Where did you *come* from? How long had you been up here, hiding in the shadows every time you heard a noise? Days? Weeks? *Years?*

No, don't try to answer. Your throat was never meant for speech. It doesn't really matter, anyway. You might have stayed up here for ever and we'd never have met.

But we *did*.

And that was when *everything* changed.

I didn't know *what* to make of you at first. I'd never seen anything like you before. Your eyes so big, black and frightened, your skin so *wet*-looking in the torchlight. I didn't know whether or not to be afraid. I suppose I would have killed you there and then if you'd been smaller and I could have stepped on you.

But then I noticed something else in your eyes, some other emotion, something I felt I could identify with. And when I saw *that*, the answers to my questions seemed unimportant.

All that mattered was that you were *here*.

It took time to overcome your shyness, do you remember? Mine, too, I suppose, although I had been out with a girl, once before.

Did I ever tell you about Carla? I

named you after her, you know. About thirty years ago, it was. Someone Dad used to work with arranged for us to meet on a blind date. That was the only reason she turned up.

Anyway, the date itself was a bit of a disaster. We had nothing at all in common. She was into sports. I wasn't. She was chatty. I've always been terrible at making conversation. She was gorgeous. I was plain and gawky.

But don't get me wrong. She was very nice and polite. So polite it was almost painful.

Well, after that I never let Dad arrange any more blind dates for me, and though I used to look at women in the street and wonder what it would be like to actually *know* one — you know, to have a wife or a girlfriend — I never had anything more than basic, everyday contact with them. Once bitten, twice shy, I suppose.

But with *us*, you and me, it was different.

Where most people would have been repelled by you, as they always are by the things they don't understand, I saw only your beauty. And where they would only ever see me as a timid, inarticulate loner, you saw me as a *man*.

We made it quite cosy up here, didn't we? The mattress, the little table, the lantern. It became our little piece of heaven. And I can't tell you how much I enjoyed those evenings we spent together, me talking to you in whispers in case my parents heard me, telling you about my life and my job down at the factory, the people I worked with, what I thought of them, what they thought of me.

And then, when I ran out of things to talk about, do you remember how we just used to sit in silence, and that time I dug out that stack of comics and annuals and read them all to you? I don't suppose you had a *clue* what I was talking about at first, but you were a quick learner. You understand me now, don't you, even though you can't answer back.

If only it could have stayed that way.

What's going through your mind right now, Carla? What are you feeling at the moment, besides fear, of course? Anger? Relief? Sorrow? *Guilt?*

You never should have gone downstairs, you know. All right, all right, I know we've been through it a dozen times, but . . . you shouldn't have. You *know* it was wrong. And look how it ended.

Why did you go down there in the first place, anyway? What were you looking for? *Me*? But you *knew* I was at work . . .

All right, Carla. I'm sorry. *Please* stop crying. All I'm saying is, surely you knew that if you left the loft you'd be seen?

And you *were* seen.

I'll never forget that phone call at work. 'Ted, come home quickly, your father's had an accident.'

Can you imagine it?

The journey home seemed to take forever, and by the time I got in I was sweating like a pig. The ambulance men were already here by then, of course, though a fat lot of good they were. One of them told me that Dad had fallen down the stairs and broken his neck.

He was dead.

At first, we thought he'd slipped. I mean, he was well into his seventies, and frail with it. But then I noticed that sparkling trail running down the wall beneath the loft-hatch.

I followed it down to the landing carpet. It looked like you'd circled around for a while, searching. *Looking for me*.

That was when I knew what had *really* happened.

I saw it all in my mind, like a scene from a film. You'd come down from the loft, though how you managed to ease open the hatch I'll never know, and while you were on the landing, Dad had come up the stairs and seen you.

But for God's sake, Carla, he wasn't *like* me! He was too *old* for shocks.

He must have stumbled backward and fallen.

And died.

It should have ended there. I should have seen our relationship for the unnatural, unclean thing it was: that flesh that was smooth and flesh that was scaled should never have mixed.

It was like a nightmare, and yet, God help me, I still loved you. I loved you too much to end it. I lay in bed every night, listening to you sliding desperately over the floorboards above me. That and mother crying in the next bedroom.

And I kept imagining what it must have been like for Dad, what he must have felt when he saw you and stepped back in horror. I could almost *feel* that terrible sense of panic when he realised he'd stepped back into nothing more substantial than thin air, and the crack of his neck snapping echoed in my dreams and woke me in a cold sweat more than once.

That was why we had to move, Mum and me. I couldn't see any other way out of it. I still loved you, but now I knew that our love was never meant to be, so I suggested to Mum that we sell the house and find something smaller, where she wouldn't be reminded of Dad's . . . *accident* . . . and she agreed. We put the house up for sale and eventually it was bought by a family named Glover.

You knew what was happening, didn't you, when I started clearing out the loft. You *guessed*. And though I never meant to hurt you, I had to ignore you, Carla, I had to pretend you weren't there, because if I'd once looked in your direction, into your face, into your eyes, then I knew it would start up all over again, and I really didn't want that.

Mum and I moved into a bungalow. It wasn't very far away, but far *enough*, I hoped. But distance had nothing to do with it. If anything, it only made things *worse*, because everywhere I went, I began to notice the way people *looked* at me again. Being with you, I'd forgotten what that was like. At least when we'd been together, you made me feel *normal*.

I had to see you again, and I was a fool to ever think otherwise. When you love someone as I loved you, you couldn't just walk out on them and expect it to end as suddenly as that. I could neither eat nor sleep for thinking of you. I pictured you all alone in that musty old loft, easing yourself aimlessly around, waiting for me to come back and knowing in your heart that I never would.

But it was too late. The house had been sold and the new owners had moved in. Even though I desperately needed to see you again, it was impossible.

Except . . .

Except that I still had a key to the back door.

I suppose I knew all along why I'd kept it, even if I didn't want to admit it to myself. And though the Glovers might have changed the locks on the front door, I doubted very much that they'd have bothered with the back.

Still, how could I break into the house, get you out of the loft and somehow take you back home with me? The only possible way would be under cover of darkness, and when the house was empty. But I had to base my plans around the Glovers' movements. So I took some time off work, and over the next two weeks started making notes.

Mr Glover left the house every weekday morning at eight o'clock sharp. His two children left half an hour later. Mrs Glover didn't appear to have a job. She did her shopping twice a week, on Tuesdays and Thursdays, usually between eleven and half-past twelve. On Wednesday afternoons she went out between two and half-past four, and because she was always smartly dressed, I assumed she went to visit a friend or relation, maybe even a fancy-man.

On Thursday evenings, the whole family went out together, usually at seven o'clock. They came home between ten and half-past.

By the start of the fourth week, I had decided on a plan. I would break into the house on Thursday evening, bring you down from the loft and take you home hidden in a sack or something. I knew I was taking a chance, that I'd be breaking the law, but I was so desperate by then that any risk seemed worth it.

That Thursday evening I parked the car a few streets away and walked the rest of the way, slowly, to kill time. I couldn't get you out of my mind, because a new thought had started nagging at me: whether or not you'd managed to escape detection by the Glovers. I thought you probably *had*, otherwise there would have been something in the papers about it, but I couldn't be sure.

The streets were cold and quiet. It was November, and the early evening was mercifully dark. When I arrived at the house, it was silent. I went up the path and rang the doorbell, just to make sure no-one was home. I had a story worked out in case anyone answered the door, but no-one did.

I looked to left and right. The street was empty. Not stopping to think about it, I quickly disappeared down the alley between the house and its next-door neighbour, clambered over the fence and waited, crouched in the shadows, until my heavy breathing returned to something like normal.

The place was lit by moonlight. I could see that they'd done a few things with the garden: we'd never bothered ourselves.

I was terrified.

I waited at the back door for fifteen minutes until I felt confident enough to actually do what I'd set out to do. I had trouble fitting the key in the lock, because my hands were trembling from a mixture of fear and the cold, but finally it slid in and I turned it, hoping to God that they hadn't fitted any bolts since they'd moved in.

They hadn't.

I let myself in and closed but didn't lock the door behind me. My breathing sounded even louder now, so loud that I felt sure that someone outside would hear it and call the police. It was only my imagination, of course, but that's the way fear makes you think.

I waited for my eyes to adjust to the darkness, then picked my way through the kitchen, through the dining room, out into the hallway and up the stairs.

On the landing, I thought I heard you slithering about overhead. No-one else would ever notice it, of course: they wouldn't know what to listen out for. It was a relief to know that you were still here.

I paused, making sure there were no other sounds. Then I looked up at the loft hatch, and it was only then that I realised I had no way to reach it.

I'd always kept a stepladder in the spare bedroom when we lived there. It hadn't occurred to me how I would get to the hatch now. An awful sense of despair washed through me. You were so close, but just out of reach.

Then I saw the chest of drawers. It was a neat little piece of furniture, and it was sturdy enough to take my weight. I dragged it across to a spot beneath the hatch, climbed onto it, opened the hatch and drew down the loft-ladder.

A minute or two later I was there, in the loft itself, running my torch to right and left. I couldn't see you anywhere, and I felt panic rising as I wondered whether something bad had happened to you after all.

But then I saw that familiar glistening trail and followed it back to the spot where I'd first found you.

Oh, Carla.

I can still see the way the tears shone against your silver skin, and I think I loved you more in that moment than at any time before or since.

But we never should have done the terrible thing we did.

I couldn't get it out of my mind afterwards. I'm not even sure I *wanted* to.

Until now.

How long were we together? An hour

or so? And then a key rattled in the lock and the front door swung open.

Oh, Christ.

How can you describe what happens to you at a moment like that? I felt sick, panicky, like it was all over. There was regret, too, because I knew I shouldn't have wasted so much time, I should have gotten you out of there and left straight away.

But we'd taken our time instead, and now it looked as if we'd be caught.

I didn't think I could stand to have the whole story made public.

I crouched by the open hatch, listened to the muted sounds of conversation coming from the hallway below. *Of all the times to come home early* —

I heard lights being switched on. A kettle boiled, a cistern flushed. Then they — the Glovers, I mean — switched on their television and closed the living room door and I felt weak with relief, because we hadn't been discovered — *yet*.

Still, I knew I couldn't take you with me now, and much as I hated to leave you there, I didn't see what else I could do but leave you behind. It was going to be hard enough for me to get out of the house alone, now that they'd come home. At least if I could get out undetected, there was a chance I could come back for you at a later date.

I descended the ladder, closed it up and pushed it up into the darkness. Then I climbed onto the chest of drawers, closed the hatch and manhandled the chest back to its original position. Peering over the banister, I made sure the Glovers were all still in the living room, then I began to creep downstairs, one step at a time, holding my breath until I thought I would burst.

It took forever. But at last I reached the bottom. The sound of the television was louder now: loud enough, hopefully, to cover any noises I might make getting out of there.

I eased past the living room door, fighting the urge to run. Then I slipped back through the dining room and into the kitchen.

I don't know how it happened. I think I bumped into a cabinet and knocked a vase or a figurine to the floor. I remember panicking, then racing blindly for the back door and catching my leg on a chair. A door opened, light shone in the hallway. I heard voices, footsteps, and I couldn't help it: I wet myself.

I tore open the back door and ran, and to this day I don't remember a thing about going over the garden fence or back along the alleyway. I ran up the street even as the front door opened and someone started shouting. Footsteps rang on the pavement behind me: someone grabbed my sleeve and I pushed them away, desperation giving me strength and the courage to use it. Whoever grabbed me fell backwards.

When I got home I was sick with fright. Had they seen me? Did they recognise me? Had I made sure the hatch was shut? What about fingerprints?

For the next week solid, I worried myself sick.

But nothing happened. They hadn't recognised me. I was safe.

There was a problem, though. They'd be changing locks and fitting bolts now.

Trying to get in through the back door again was out of the question.

I racked my brains to come up with another plan, but there was no way I could hope to get you out of there unless the house was empty. If this had been summer, they might have been planning a holiday. But we were four weeks away from Christmas, and I didn't think they'd be going away for a while yet, and certainly not for any length of time.

In any case, how could I get back into the house if they changed the locks on the back door, as they were bound to do?

It might take some time to work it all out, but I would come back for you eventually. Meanwhile, I had to see you again and explain what had happened. At least then you'd know that I hadn't deserted you for good.

The thought of going back to the house scared me, but there was no way around it, so a fortnight later I called on Mrs Glover. She remembered me from the sale of the house and invited me in. I told her that I had lost a ring, and the last time I remembered wearing it was when

I'd cleared out the loft shortly before we moved. I wondered if it would be possible for me to have a quick look up there now, just to see if I could find it.

I didn't miss the look she gave me. She didn't want a stranger nosing around her house, but she took pity on me. She said she'd go and get the stepladder out.

Fortunately, she left me to it. I'd had an idea she would. Like most people, she probably thought that lofts were filled with dust and spiders. I could hear her humming pleasantly in the kitchen as I stepped into the darkness and switched on the torch she'd given me.

But something was wrong. This time, you hadn't made any attempt to hide. You just lay on your mattress, looking feverish and sick. I could see it — as I saw so much — in your eyes.

And your stomach . . .

I thought at first that you'd caught some kind of disease and were dying, but then I went cold because I realised that the truth was even worse.

You were pregnant.

The colour drained from my face, and

though our eyes locked, I knew you didn't even recognise me. While I tried to get over the shock, I pulled the mattress over to the far corner, behind the chimney breast, and then went back downstairs. I told Mrs Glover I hadn't been able to find my fictitious ring and went straight home.

The more I thought about what we'd done, the more I just wanted to curl up and die. It seemed as if our love had caused nothing but trouble. It had caused the death of my father and turned me into a lawbreaker and a liar. And now this . . .

What would our children look like, Carla? *You? Me?* Or a mixture of *both* of us? Whichever way it turned out, one thing was certain. They wouldn't be *right*. All we could bring into the world were freaks.

If I felt desperate before, it was as nothing to how I felt now. I thought at first that there still might be a way out, that perhaps we could wait until the, uh, *baby*, was born, and then drown it or something, but somehow I knew you would never allow that.

I could see that in your eyes, too. But

don't worry, I understand. It's only natural.

In any case, I think I knew all along that it would end like this. I just didn't want to admit it. But in the end, it got so that I just couldn't stand it any more. Anything was better than the living hell I was putting myself through. I wanted the two of us to be together, but I couldn't take the responsibility of bringing some kind of *mutation* into the world.

So we *have* to die, Carla. Even more so now that you've already given birth to . . . *them*.

Look at them, Carla. Seven lumps of twitching, flexing flesh: armless, legless, hairless, unable even to cry the way babies do. They're *freaks*, Carla, they were never *meant* to live, and soon they'll die, as well.

I think Mrs Glover will be all right. I had to hit her, you see. It was the only way I could get back in here to do . . . what has to be done. I left her on the sofa in the living room. By the time she wakes up, it should all be over.

You're looking at the gun, aren't you,

wondering where I got it.

There's a bloke at work who collects Second World War memorabilia, Nazi uniforms and badges, that sort of thing. I told him I was thinking of starting a collection of my own and asked him if he could get me a gun to kick off with. Not the kind where they block up the barrel and remove the firing pin. I told him I wanted the real thing.

Anyway, he knows a man who knows a man, another collector, I think. He got me the gun and the ammunition. Cost me two hundred pounds, but he says that's dirt cheap. He tells me it's a Walther P38, a real collector's item.

Well, enough talk. This is it.

I suppose I've been going on like this just to delay it for as long as possible. But it's best to get it over and done with, now.

Hold still, Carla. I'll try to make this as quick and painless as I can.

That's it. Good girl. Hold still, so I can put the barrel to your head.

Goodbye, Carla. I love you.

God help me, Carla, *I love you so much*.

The Thirteenth Dream

Red mist swirled around him like living silk. Black, brittle grass crackled underfoot. And even though he kept telling himself that there was nothing to be scared of, that he was only dreaming, even though he *knew* it was just a dream, Andrew Crane was still afraid. He could feel the cool kiss of the mist against his skin, and smell the sulphur hanging in the moist air, and these things told him that it was much *more* than a dream. And possibly much *worse*.

He turned slowly, straining his eyes to see beyond the shifting crimson veil. He could make out nothing but an eternal, starless night, through which strange things flew: three-winged animals with fins and scales that were gone almost before he knew they were there.

Where am I? Why am I here? Why am I dreaming about . . . this?

He shivered.

Then he heard voices.

There were two of them, and they came from everywhere and yet nowhere. They sounded like the dry crackle of dead autumn leaves and the papery rasp of reptilian scales across stone. They could have been male or female or some mixture of the two, but of one thing he was certain: they were unimaginably *old*.

You are full of doubt, said the first.

Uncertain, said the second.

Worried.

Unhappy.

Frustrated.

Crane felt sweat drying against his top lip. His dark eyes bulged as he tried to see beyond the mist and find the speakers, but it was impossible. The voices circled him like elusive, slithering animals. They could have come from anywhere, and yet he had the coldest feeling that they were actually coming from *inside* him.

We can help you, the first voice whispered.

And we will — eventually, said the second.

When you are ready to accept our . . . terms.

For the first time, Crane managed to find his voice. 'Who . . . I don't understand. Who are you? *Where* are you?'

There was a pause before the first voice said, *We are here. That is all you need to know.*

You will know when and how to summon us, added the second. *Do not doubt that we shall answer.*

Crane was about to say more but stopped, sensing that they — whoever *they* were — were leaving. He waited for one stretched second, straining his ears to catch the last of their whisperings, the red mist rising and falling before his eyes as if propelled by some demonic heartbeat. And then, so faintly that he almost didn't hear it, the two sexless voices joined to give one soft, final prophesy:

Thrice the Devil Snake hath screamed,
And so our Master hath it deemed,
To make the fated seek our aid,
A hellish Goblin must be made.

Again he heard the awful sound of beating wings above him, felt the mist cling to his skin, began to choke as it filled in nostrils —

And then he woke up.

Terrified.

He didn't start work until late the following morning, putting it off for as long as he could, writing emails, sending texts, making phone calls, walking the grounds that surrounded his house. But then, as always, he found that he could put it off no longer.

Reluctantly he left the house and made his way along the wide stone path that led to the studio. He'd had it built two years earlier, when he'd been at the height of his career, and the *enfant terrible* of the art world. He was only thirty four now, of course, but he knew he would never again create the kind of works that had established him as a major talent. No. Those days were long gone.

Reaching the studio, he paused for a moment in the doorway, looking around, his eyes settling for one guilty second on the workbench, then drifting away. It was a large studio, built on two levels, the lowest serving as temporary living quarters for whenever he worked late and couldn't be bothered to go back to the house, the highest, where fresh sunlight streamed down through the ornate skylight, the area where he actually worked.

Except that he *didn't* work anymore.

He crossed the room and fixed a cup of coffee, just to delay the inevitable a while longer.

How long had it been now since he'd done anything really worthwhile? Six months? Eight?

Longer.

He had simply woken up one morning and realised that whatever talent he possessed was gone.

There had been no tears, no tantrums — just a calm realisation that he had lost all feeling for his work. The heartache came later, when that terrible mixture of emptiness and impotence finally struck him. The panic had set in then, when he had started project after project in a feverish attempt to regain it, all to no avail.

As he sipped his coffee, he wondered again if talent, *real* talent, could vanish as quickly as his had. Had there ever been talent there to begin with, or had it all just been plain, daft luck, a case of his being in the right place at the right time?

Abruptly he set the mug down and studied the workbench. Biting at his lower lip, trying to ignore the quivering in his guts, he approached it slowly, as if it might spring to life if disturbed. He scooped a lump of clay from the bin beside it, slapped it against the workbench a few times to knock the air bubbles out of it.

Thrice the Devil Snake hath screamed . . .

He swore softly.

And now, he thought, *these fucking nightmares*.

For the past twelve nights he had dreamed himself into the same vivid scene: a dark, featureless plain with black grass beneath him and a starless night sky above, and all around him swirling red mist. But last night had been different. Last night there had been voices.

He shivered at the memory, slapping

the clay against the bench harder than he needed to. He was under pressure from his agent and his business manager to mount a new exhibition, the only things he'd managed to finish looked more like the immature works of a disinterested schoolboy, and now even his sleep was being disturbed. His whole life was falling apart and it wasn't fair!

With effort he stifled the urge to scream and forced himself to work diligently for the next twenty minutes, his once-deft fingers now moving awkwardly over the clay like those of a blind man feeling his way across unfamiliar terrain. The sun slid across the sky and shadows began to grow. The room was silent for a long time.

And then the air was torn by a cry of pure anguish and Crane threw the formless clay across the room. He fell to his knees, his slim hands held before him but washed from his vision by angry tears. There was nothing in them: no feeling, no inspiration, no talent, *nothing!*

Great agonising sobs shook him as he curled into a ball. His hands folded into fists and he beat at the floor in frustration.

Gradually the blows grew weaker. The sun sank lower. Soon it was night.

The *thirteenth* night.

And so our Master hath it deemed, to make the Fated seek our aid . . .

He dragged himself to his feet, exhausted by emotion, and stumbled from the darkened studio. The cool night air made his red eyes sting but couldn't clear his mind of the screaming doubts that filled it. He staggered blindly into the house, at last came to the dining room and almost tore the top off a bottle of Bushmills. He filled a tumbler and emptied it desperately, choking as the fire slid down into his belly.

Taking the bottle with him into the lounge, he built a fire in the hearth. When it was blazing and he had drawn the curtains to shut out the night, he fell into a chair and poured another drink. He didn't want to think about it anymore but still his mind kept asking why, why, *why?*

Could talent just disappear? If so, *why?* Was he trying too hard, or not hard *enough?* Should he have to try at *all?* Shouldn't he just let it all happen naturally? That's how it had always been in the past. Yes, it had all come naturally then. But now . . .

He shook his head. Now, nothing came naturally. Except —

He spilled more whiskey into his glass.

Except this.

Outside, the moon rose and the stars came out. A playful breeze whispered through the trees and ruffled the grass with cold fingers. It carried a few specks of rain with it and threw them tapping at the windows, but Crane never heard them. He had fallen into a deep, drunken slumber.

Swirling red mist advanced across the lawn.

When he opened his eyes, he knew — *hoped* — he was dreaming. Brittle black grass lay fragile beneath his feet. Beyond the restless red mist lay only eternal, starless night.

I'm dreaming, I'm drunk, I —

Do you now seek our aid? asked a voice.

Crane shook his head, trying to clear it. 'Who . . . who are you? *Where* are you?'

Do you now seek our aid? asked the old-as-time voice again. It displayed neither patience nor impatience, but allowed his imagination to colour the words.

'What do you mean?' he asked.

Your talent, whispered the second voice.

He searched in vain for the speakers, sulphur making the breath catch in his throat. 'I don't *have* any talent,' he said in disgust.

Your talent is great, the first dry voice contradicted.

'You're wrong.'

We are seldom wrong.

'Well, you're wrong this time.'

Are we?

Silence pressed in on him, threatening to crush his ears and fill his nose, to choke him and leave him cold and dead on this strange black plain, food for nameless creatures and maybe worse.

Do you now seek our aid? repeated the first voice.

Crane stared into the mist. 'Where are you?'

We are here, said the first voice. *That is enough.*

'*Tell me!*' he shouted.

There was no echo, only more awful silence and a terrible, skin-tingling feeling of loneliness.

'Come back,' he breathed to the red, restless mist.

In some nameless way he felt their return.

Then you do *seek our aid?*

He nodded desperately. 'Yes,' he

murmured, low and ashamed.

There is a price, said the first voice.

'Name it.'

There is no currency with which you could pay the price we demand, said the second voice.

What use have we for money? asked the first voice. *We, who were banished and all but forgotten by your kind?*

The voices circled him, rising and falling, hissing and spitting.

Crane cleared his throat. 'Then what is your price?' he croaked.

There was a long pause. Then the first hermaphroditic voice whispered, *That you . . . obey us*.

Crane frowned. 'Obey? But what — '

Obey, said the first voice, but said no more.

'You must tell me more,' he urged.

Can it be that the whelp makes demands? asked the second voice, and now the outrage was clear in its chilly tones.

He will learn, predicted the first.

Crane shook his head in bafflement. 'You have to tell me more! You can hardly expect me to sign my life away without knowing what's expected of me!'

After a moment, the first voice allowed, *There is more, but at this stage it is . . . unimportant.*

He was afraid to ask more lest he anger them again.

Now, whelp, your answer, demanded the second voice.

Yea or nay? asked the first.

Crane hesitated. This was madness, all of it, just a crazy dream, a nightmare. It was, damn it, it *was* . . .

But he said, 'I accept.'

There was a pause before the first voice remarked, *You were . . . wise.*

But remember, whelp, said the second voice. *You have entered willingly into a contract with us and you are bound to it by the very thickness of your blood. Were you at any time to consider breaking your word . . .*

The voice trailed off.

'It's all right,' Crane said tiredly. 'I understand.'

He felt them leave him then, though he could not say how. And, as before, their final words circled him like phantom carousel horses.

Even as we sing this song,
From this night forth and from now on,
Your skills will be their very best,
Our guarantee a year-long test

The world around him went black.

Andrew Crane's return to prominence came like the answer to a prayer. From the morning after the thirteenth dream, he approached his work like a man inspired. For the first time in too long, there was nothing to stand in his way, no blocks, no doubts, no fears. And the *ideas!* They seemed to flow endlessly, almost too many to handle. But always they felt just right. The dry spell was over, thank God.

During the first three months he produced some of his finest work, toiling long hours without complaint as his slim fingers flashed with a will of their own, creating image after image, statement after statement. After five months he was able to mount a new exhibition at the Malvern Gallery which met with tremendous success. Time and again he appeared in the arts pages as each new piece sold for a record sum.

Occasionally he recalled the weird crimson dreams, but rarely did he dwell on them. They were only dreams, after all: they meant nothing.

In any case, all that really mattered to him was happening right now. He was riding high, creating things that were worth creating, and his only reason for climbing out of bed every morning was simply in order to create more.

One fine spring morning just over a year later, he woke early, showered, dressed, skipped breakfast and hurried out to the studio. Work on his latest sculpture had been going well and he was in an exceptionally good mood. Never before had he felt such satisfaction from a project, and he was anxious to get back to it.

Nature was waking up all around him and before he disappeared into the studio he paused to smell the freshness of the air and listen to the birdsong in the nearby trees. He had never felt so completely alive, and life was good.

He turned and went into the studio.

Birds sang. Insects buzzed.

And five minutes later, Andrew Crane screamed.

Move, damn you, move! As he tried to flex his frozen fingers, he could barely stifle a sob of terror. He was shaking badly and his face was slick with sweat.

Move, damn you, move!

But it was no good. Despite all his efforts, his hands remained stubbornly locked.

He collapsed into a chair, staring down at them as if seeing them for the first time, lifting them slowly until they were held trembling before him. There was nothing wrong with them that he could see. Nothing wrong with them that he could feel. He just couldn't *use* them.

Frantically, awkwardly, he tried to massage some feeling back into them, trying not to think about what this might mean. He kept rubbing them, hoping for a blessed sensation of pins and needles that wouldn't come. He screamed at them to move, but they remained paralysed.

Paralysed. The word sent a shiver through him, and half-baked ideas about just what multiple sclerosis and muscular dystrophy were, and words like *stroke*, suddenly announced themselves in his mind.

Oh God, please no . . . Fear and bitterness threatened to choke him as he shook his head. *Oh no . . .*

Abruptly he came back down to earth. The studio around him was absolutely silent.

Somehow he managed to wipe the mess of sweat and tears from his cheeks, screwed his eyes shut and drew down several deep breaths in an effort to calm himself. Gradually he felt the pounding of his pulses slow, the beat of his heart settle. When he felt better, he began again, staring down at the fixed hands before him as a voice inside him begged, *Move . . . move . . .* please *move . . .*

At the end of an hour he could just about move the tips of his fingers, and for the first time since it had happened he felt a pathetic surge of hope. But what had caused them to freeze in the first place? Yesterday, this morning when he had woken up, his hands had been fine. It was only when he'd started to work that the pain had ripped through them, leaving them numb and useless.

Move . . . move . . . move . . .

By noon he was exhausted, but at least his hands had come back to life. He could use them for almost everything — opening books and cupboards, picking up pens and writing neatly. But as soon as he tried to work the clay he felt the paralysis creeping back into them.

Panic seized him again then, the same blind panic of a year before that he had all but forgotten, and as he recalled it, so too he remembered the dreams and the words that had been spoken therein.

Your skills will now be at their best,
Our guarantee a year-long test . . .

He looked at his hands for a long time.

A year-long test . . .

But it was only a dream, he thought, a dream, *for Christ's sake!*

Grimly he forced movement into the

locked fingers until they clawed at the air like fat spider's legs, but every time he attempted to work the clay they froze again, as if they had been cursed.

Which, of course, they had.

Luckily, Crane was able to keep his visit to the specialist a secret, even from those closest to him. If something like this got out, his existing works would soar in value . . . but anything he was able to produce subsequently would always be subject to even closer scrutiny.

He arrived quietly at the office of Dr Geeta Sudra at exactly ten o'clock on a bright but chilly April morning two days after that first attack, and sat with forced patience as his hands and lower back were X-rayed and then examined with the greatest care. Blood was drawn and analysed. A CT scan was taken of his head, then a series of minute electric shocks were sent through his hands. At three o'clock that afternoon Dr Sudra, a petite woman who looked far too young to be the world-class neuropathologist she was, ran gold-flecked eyes over the findings, mentioned terms like CBC and blood differential, electromyography and nerve conduction velocity, and then shook her head.

'There is no disturbance in your immune system,' she reported. 'No inflammation of the blood vessels, and aside from the attacks which brought you here in the first place, absolutely no loss of muscle function. All of which leads me to believe that your problem is not so much physical as psychological.'

'In other words,' Crane said bitterly, 'you're saying I'm mad.'

'I'm suggesting that you see a psychiatrist,' replied the doctor. 'It's not quite the same thing.'

A few discreet enquiries later, Crane went to see Dr Vernon Moffat, and in quiet but opulent surroundings reluctantly confessed everything: of his agonising period of being unable to create, of the weird dreams and the bargain he had made within them, of the following year of almost unprecedented success and now, his inability to even *touch* clay without rendering his hands immobile.

Dr Moffat nodded sympathetically

whenever Crane's eyes fell on him. He jotted notes on a pad and then gave the matter some deep thought. At last he prescribed a complete break from work.

'Do whatever you like,' he said. 'Take a cruise, *anything*. But don't even *think* about work for at least two months.'

Seeing Crane frown, he leaned forward across his desk. He smelled of rich cigars and mothballs. 'This sort of thing is not at all uncommon, Mr Crane. By your own admission, you have just been through your most creative spell to date. There is nothing wrong with you that I can see, either physically or mentally. You have simply overloaded your creative circuits.'

He sat back again, smiling at the phrase. 'I have them all in here, you know: writers, actors, captains of industry. It's because their careers demand so much from them that they quite often feel they have reached a point beyond which, creatively, they can give no more.'

He stabbed at the air with one fat index finger. 'It is at this point that a complete break is absolutely vital, and only after such a rest is it possible for them to find the confidence to go back to the business of being creative.' He spread his hands. 'It works every time.'

Crane shifted irritably in his chair. 'But what about the dreams?' he asked.

Moffat toyed with his expensive gold fountain pen. 'They were your mind's way of dealing with the problem when it first arose,' he explained smoothly. 'By acting out this bizarre ritual every night, you were able to overcome your creative block. And so you did, for one year.

'But now that year is up, and you really *do* need a rest. In fact, your subconscious is *insisting* upon it. That's why it won't allow you to use your hands for any but the most mundane tasks.'

He narrowed his eyes. He could tell he hadn't quite convinced Crane, so he smiled again. 'Just you take it from me,' he urged pleasantly.

Reluctantly, Crane did.

That night he sprawled by the fire, tumbler in hand, idly watching the patterns thrown up by the dancing flames. He had given the matter considerable thought and decided to take the psychiatrist's advice. After all, he could hardly remember the last time he'd taken a break. And, though he was reluctant to admit it, he *was* exhausted. It was just that, up until now, he'd felt so alive and charged with ability that he'd never wanted to rest.

Still, it seemed as if his mind had been made up for him. He flexed his fingers, watched them move easily for a moment, then sat forward, poured himself another drink, took a sip and set the tumbler down on the coffee table at his side.

In a way, he was almost looking forward to a break. The fire warmed him and he closed his eyes, allowing his thoughts to drift. As the whiskey settled inside him he felt his muscles relax. He stretched his legs out, listening idly to the crackle of the fire, and for the first time in days felt content. Everything was going to be all right.

Gradually his breathing grew heavier and his fingers began to twitch. His eyes, beneath their closed lids, began to roll.

He was asleep.

And dreaming.

The first thing he became aware of was the smell of sulphur, and when he opened his eyes he saw red mist dancing before him like smoke dyed in blood.

He looked around. It was incredible. Nothing had changed. Everything was as it had been before. And it was all so *vivid*. No star shone down from the ebon sky, no moon reflected in the dull surface of the dead grass beneath his feet. The only light appeared to come from the mist itself, which glowed like a fresh wound.

He shook his head in a mixture of disbelief and denial. He couldn't accept that it was a dream, not now that he was actually here again. So much about it seemed real, so many of his senses told him it was actually happening.

Clearing his throat, he finally summoned the courage to call tentatively, 'Hello?'

There came no reply, and yet somehow

he could feel their presence, sense them watching him from great, unscalable heights. He raised his voice again. 'Hello?'

His words were swallowed by the hungry darkness.

Then:

And so we are joined once more, said a voice, dry like the most pitiless desert.

The breath caught sharply in his throat as he scanned the fog, knowing full well that he would not see the speaker unless he/she/it wished to be seen.

Fighting to get the words past the lump in his throat, he said, 'Yes. I . . . As you promised, I have been . . . able.'

He sensed the nodding of an aged head. *We kept our part of the bargain*, the voice agreed.

'You did,' Crane said to the restless red air. 'But you broke it as well. I'm useless again.'

There was a pause. *No*, said the voice at last.

Without warning, Crane's temper flared. 'Yes, damn you! *Useless!*'

No, the voice repeated calmly. *Your abilities are unimpaired. But we gave you twelve months in which to enjoy them. Now that period has ended, we have merely reminded you that the time has come for the price to be paid.*

Crane nodded slowly. 'So you turned me into a cripple,' he said, lifting his hands and turning them slowly.

The affliction is but temporary, the voice said reasonably.

When it said no more, Crane asked, 'What do you want me to do, then?'

There was another pause, longer than the first. Then the second ancient voice spoke. *You will make for us one image every twelve-month.*

Crane frowned. 'Image? You mean a *sculpture?*'

Again he sensed the nodding of wise heads.

'What type of . . . image?' he asked.

You will be told.

'When?'

Soon.

'Well, will it be large, small, hard, easy? Will it cost much to make?'

It will be small, said the first withered voice. *By your standards. It will cost little and for someone of your talent it will be easy. If you obey our instructions.*

'And you want one such sculpture every year?'

No two will be alike, said the second voice.

'And in return,' said Crane, 'I will be able to use my hands again?'

Your hands will not fail you while ever you are faithful to us, said the first voice.

Crane opened his mouth to say more but felt the cold air tremble against his skin and knew that the unseen beings were taking their leave of him. Fading, fading, all but the smallest whisper, he just managed to hear their parting chant before he collapsed.

We summoned you to keep your word,
And human pup, now you have heard,
To our cry you'll lend an ear,
And sculpt for us one child each year.

It was with more than a little trepidation that Crane set to work the following morning. The day was bright and dry but the nylon-reinforced clay felt cold and damp like corpse-flesh to his palms and, unsettled, he turned on the radio to fill the empty air.

He studied the clay with morbid fascination for some time before finding the courage to touch it again. The memory of his frozen hands was still fresh in his mind and though he had spent most of the night telling himself that he had only been dreaming, some half-forgotten sense buried deep inside him told him he was wrong. It was real, all of it. As incredible as it was, it *had happened*.

He bit his lip. The idea of taking a break suddenly seemed more attractive than ever. But something within him, some instinct that even he couldn't explain, told him that it would do no good to run. Not from them.

At last he set his palms against the cold clay, let them rest there for a moment, ready to pull them away the instant he felt the paralysis creeping back into them. But nothing happened. He let his breath out in a long, cautious sigh. A moment later he began to work the clay.

His hands scrabbled across its surface like two albino rats, shaping, stroking, styling. He wasn't really working on anything particular, just testing to see if he could use his hands again, as the dream-beings had promised.

Before five minutes had passed he was laughing and crying and laughing again. His hands felt marvellous! And that meant he could work again, *create* again!

He clapped them together and the crack they made brought him back to his senses. His face clouded. Slowly he lifte his hands. They were stained with c and very much alive. He flexed ther the warmth and life and talen them.

Oh, he had questions, of co

But he knew better than to ask them.

Instead he let his hands drop to his sides. Who needed answers, anyway? Were they so important? Suddenly he didn't think so. Nothing mattered apart from being able to create. *Nothing*. And as long as he *could* create, there would be no questions asked.

No questions at all.

But even as the sun began to sink and the afternoon turned to evening, and artificial daylight bulbs shone down on the workbench and threw long shadows around the rest of the studio, Crane began to realise that something in the room was not quite *right*.

He glanced around. It was nothing he could put his finger on, just a vague sense of unease, something that made his skin crawl and gave him the feeling he was being watched. He peered into the surrounding gloom for a time: then, realising just how much his back and neck ached, began to stretch.

And that was when he heard them.

He froze, his eyes widening. *What the* —

Whispers flew through the air, obscene and ancient words that were never meant for human ears. Crane's eyes darted to every corner, saw nothing out of the ordinary. He jerked around when he felt some presence behind him, sagged with relief when he realised he was alone.

But *still* he heard them. Yelps and whinnies and screams and cries shot toward him like poisoned arrows, and he lifted one clay-stained hand to his mouth and bit at it nervously. He tried to speak but nothing came out. His legs felt weak, his stomach churned —

And then he saw red mist spilling slowly through the cracks at the doors and windows, filling the room and staining the air the colour of hell. He watched with bug-eyed fascination, his face shining with sweat, his feet rooted to the spot by fear.

He heard — or *thought* he heard — something behind him, spun again, came abruptly to a halt and half-choked on a sob of pure terror as he came face to face with two large figures, seen dimly through the fog.

They stood eight feet tall, their bodies hidden beneath long scarlet cloaks, their faces — if faces they had — lost beneath the shadows thrown by their voluminous hoods. They stood motionless, silent, and even though he could not see them, he felt their dead red eyes burning into him.

He shook his head, trying to banish them from sight. 'A dream,' he said in a hollow whisper. 'It's a dream.'

It is no dream, said one of the figures in a sexless voice he recognised immediately, and there was something in the way it was said that made him realise once and for all that it *wasn't* a dream, and that it never had been.

You will begin, said the first figure.

Now, said the second.

Crane shuddered. 'Begin what? Your sculpture?'

They stared at him from beneath their shadowed hoods, their silence the silence of a graveyard shunned even by the dead. Then, very deliberately, one of them nodded.

We require a . . . likeness.

'A likeness of what?' Crane asked hoarsely.

The second figure said flatly, *Skarasis*.

'What? I don't understand. What is Skarasis?'

Our son, the first figure said heavily.

He has been absent for too long, said the second.

He realised then that they would offer no more information unless he asked for it. Feverishly he said, 'How will I know what . . . what he looked like? Will you describe him to me, or what?'

We will help you, said the first figure.

Advise you.

Show you engravings.

The resemblance must be absolute, stressed the second figure. *Complete in both dimension and likeness. It must be exact*.

Crane shook his head. 'It may take time to complete,' he muttered. He needed time to think, to take it all in.

You have two weeks, said the first figure.

Thick mist sprang up before them then, like the waters of a red fountain coming to life in slow motion, and after a moment it began to thin, until the air was clear again and the smell of sulphur just a memory.

Crane stood alone, stunned. *What's*

happening to me? What have I gotten myself into?

He turned back to the workbench and froze. There on the worktop sat five large, leather-bound books. Their covers were stained and burned, their thick, parchment pages — when at last he dared to look at them — well-thumbed and torn, each one crowded with the symbols of no language he had ever seen. The alien text was broken every few pages by diagrams and illustrations that depicted something hideous.

He took one look around the empty studio, glanced again at the books, and then, fearing the penalty for daring to disobey, began to work.

He spent the next seventy-two hours poring over the ancient drawings and sketching plans with fingers that refused to stop trembling. He ate little and drank a lot. The house sat empty, the studio silent save for the turning of brittle pages and the rat-scratching of pencils against paper. Shadows grew, shifted and lengthened as the sun rose, slid across the sky and sank below the horizon.

At length, with eyes looped by tired grey skin and cheeks shadowed with stubble, he decided that he could plan no more.

He constructed a solid armature of wire mesh to which he began to add clay. At this point he was only interested in getting the dimensions right. The fine detail would come later.

Seconds became minutes became hours as the days melted one into another. Several times he heard the door chimes jangling at the front of the house, but at no time did he make any move to answer them. On another occasion he tore the studio's telephone extension from the wall when it kept ringing. He became immersed in his work, because only by concentrating on his art could he stop his nerve from snapping altogether.

Every night the two red giants came through their scarlet haze to peer over his shoulders and watch as his pale fingers prodded the clay into shape and stroked character into its grey skin, whispering to him so softly that for all he knew the voices might have been just one voice in his head, telling him what he should add here, what he must reshape there.

As the first week drew to a close he lost himself utterly in the quest for perfection. He grew infatuated by his task, did not think to question it but lived only to complete it.

And, on the thirteenth night, complete it he did.

Standing back to admire his work, he felt suddenly anxious for the dream-beings — though why he still thought of them as such he had no idea, since they had proven to be every bit as real as he was — to arrive. He nodded thoughtfully to himself. They would approve, he was sure. How could they do otherwise? He had put everything into this sculpture, *everything*. They could hardly complain, for he had certainly not failed them.

Again he ran a critical eye over the clay figure standing before him. Instinctively he knew he should add nothing and take nothing away. It was as complete as it should be.

Skarasis.

It — *he* — stood five feet in height, his thick, scaled body bent forward slightly on short, warped legs. His seven-clawed hands were held before him as if in prayer, but the mocking idiot grin that spread across his wide mouth belied any semblance of worship.

The eyes were two round balls that bulged from lidless sockets. The nose was flat and the nostrils flared. Three small horns jutted from his sloping forehead, one above each eye and the third standing proud between them. His nipple-dotted spine ended in a long, forked tail. Huge, misshapen genitals protruded from between his legs and a rough, overlong tongue dangled loosely from between his scaly buttocks.

Crane felt a flutter of pride within him. He was beautiful!

Behind him, red mist filled the air like low, crimson clouds, and at the heart of the mist stood the two tall figures, the parents.

You have done well, said one.

Given that he was your first, said the other.

Crane turned, startled, and peered into the fog. 'You like him?' he asked softly.

The two figures studied him as the mist rose and shifted around them. One of them nodded slowly. *We do*, it admitted.

But this is only part-payment of your debt, remember. We require one such image each year.

Crane nodded obediently, a weird, loose smile hanging on his lips. He stood awkwardly before them, not sure what to do next. As if reading his mind, one of the figures stirred briefly beneath its cloak.

Go now, it said gently. *Leave us be.*

Crane glanced over his shoulder at the gargoyle. When he looked back at the beings in the mist, he did so with eyes that shone too brightly. 'I *did* it,' he whispered, his voice distant with wonder. 'I *did* it, didn't I?'

You did, the second figure replied. *And we are pleased.*

Crane felt the power of their hidden eyes burning into him. It filled him with a joy he could barely contain.

You will do great things this coming year, the first figure predicted, and Crane believed it completely.

'Thank you,' he mumbled.

Then he turned and left them alone with the image of their child.

As he stepped out into the night, cold air struck him like a fist and made him realise just how tired he was. He could hardly cling to his thoughts as he stumbled toward the house.

But he felt good. He probably looked awful, but for all that he still felt good. The creation of Skarasis had been a unique challenge, an exhilarating experience that no other artist had ever been given. Even the memory of it made him feel weak.

But God, he was tired. Absently he brushed matted hair away from his eyes. He felt as if he could sleep for a week, and yet at the same time he could hardly wait to get back to work. *You will do great things in this coming year*, they'd said. And he would. He *would!*

He paused a moment, tasting the sharp air as he stared up at the star-broken night. Shrill, joyous laughter came from the studio behind him. It sounded like glaciers crumbling.

He shivered, although he didn't feel especially cold. What he needed was a drink. He began to walk slowly toward the house again, his shadow thrown palely before him by the bloated moon above, only half-listening to the sexless voices that danced behind him.

Here he stands, our youngest son,
Given birth, for what must come . . .

Crane paused, frowning. He turned back the way he'd come. The studio glowed white in the moonlight, while the windows appeared to throb with a weird red life of their own.

With a shrug he turned away. The thought of a drink was uppermost in his mind. But then the laughter came to him again and he turned back to see exactly what was happening.

His face tightened.

The studio was half-obscured by red mist.

His frown deepened. What the hell was

going on? Instinctively he took a step back toward the studio as the voices continued to crackle through the night.

Though the eyes are dead and still,
And these, the hands, they cannot feel,
And this, the mouth, it cannot talk,
And these, the legs, refuse to walk . . .

Just what the hell were they doing?

Even as he watched, the light that shone from the studio windows seemed to dim and die as the mist grew thicker. He took another two steps forward, paused again to listen as the whispered words carried to him on the wind.

We have the power to infuse life,
We have the power to create strife,
And now we give them both to you,
As this, your flesh, transforms in hue . . .

Crane felt something snap inside him.

We have the power to infuse life . . .

Skarasis, *his* Skarasis . . .

They were bringing him to life!

He broke into a run, his footsteps

slapping against the wide stone path like seconds ticking away to midnight.

See him breathe, hear him sigh,
Listen as he gives a cry,
He recalls what he has been,
Remembers all that he has seen . . .

As he burst into the studio, Crane was enveloped by the red fog. He waved his arms frantically to disperse it. At first he could see nothing, but then he heard their shrill cackling and he turned sharply to his left.

The two scarlet figures stood facing each other, their own seven-clawed hands joined in some obscene ritual. Their long brown nails clicked together like pagan music. Their all-concealing hoods shivered with laughter. And then, suddenly, all noise and movement in them stopped.

Very slowly, the two figures separated and turned to face him. He felt smaller than ever as he stood before them, afraid even to breathe for fear of incurring their wrath.

But they did not speak. They looked at

him for a while, then turned their hidden faces away to the left. Crane stared at them for a moment longer until he realised that he should follow their gaze.

At last he found the strength to turn his head.

There, beyond the mist, he spied the statue of Skarasis, shining reptilian green, and as he watched he saw its great, scaly chest rise and fill with hot, demonic breath.

Skarasis flexed his sharp talons, the muscles beneath his skin rippling like trapped snakes. He twitched and stretched, and when he grinned he revealed a tongue as red as the fog that surrounded him, a tongue that Crane himself had fashioned from dead clay.

The round eyes rolled in their sockets, and great, rope-like veins shivered along his neck as he looked around the room.

And then Skarasis straightened to his full height and appeared to bathe in the mist, low, contented growls vibrating up from his chest with every breath of red air, and even as Crane watched, open-mouthed and shaking his head in disbelief, the mist grew thicker, thicker, until Skarasis was obscured, and the growls had died away.

The mist stirred then, as if blown by a breeze that Crane himself couldn't feel. After a moment it thinned, and when it settled to a pale, transparent crimson, he saw that Skarasis had vanished.

Heavy silence clung to the studio for a long time, until the two cloaked figures turned back to him. Feeling their hot gaze come to rest on him, he flinched.

It is done, said the first figure.

Aye, agreed the second.

Crane stared at the spot where the sculpture had been. 'Skarasis,' he whispered, and a tear left his eye.

The first figure nodded. *He is gone, whelp. But you shall hear of him again*.

The words were not meant to comfort.

We are old, said the second. *Older than this orb. We are of the Great Order, both of us mothers to the Old One, the Master. But, as I said, we are old*.

Too old to bear new children, said the first.

It is all we can do to rebirth the old,

continued the second. *Those who were banished to other, distant realms when magic was young and the Damning Spells were still remembered.*

There followed a moment of brooding silence, during which Crane looked from one to the other. Then the first figure said, *But rebirth the old we can. Summon their spirits if not their bodies from the Dark Places.*

And through you, said the second, *we can give them shells to inhabit, bodies made in the images they once possessed.*

As we have done this night with Skarasis.

And as we shall do twelve months hence for Galerial.

And then Absaloth.

And Amorion.

And so on.

Crane licked his lips, nodding his understanding. *And so on.*

Twelve months later they returned, and found Crane eager to begin his new task. It had, after all, been a good year for him and he was anxious to please his benefactors. They watched through their swirling red haze as he began his new — *their* new — creation.

Already it is forming, said the first.

Aye. More life.

The first figure turned to study its companion. Beneath the shadowy hood, its face was unreadable. *Soon we will be together again*, it remarked softly. *All of us. And the Awful Times will return.*

The second figure rubbed its claws together in anticipation. *Plagues, wars, famine, chaos . . .*

Such is what we thrive on.

And soon the whole human race will learn to worship us again.

Just as the Master foretold. Did you ever doubt?

Never.

Come, then. We still have much to do.

And this was certainly true. For many were the banished children awaiting rebirth, and one artist could never hope to play his part in the rebirthing of all of them.

They needed another.

And another.

And another . . .

Fever Pitch

4

Ashes to ashes . . .

The words stuck in my throat, too hideously apt to be said aloud. Instead, I just stood swaying in the wind, feeling the others watching me, waiting for me to go on. But what more could I say?

I hesitated for another heartbeat, listening to the dogs back in camp, barking impatiently for their food, then shook my head briefly, not looking up from the slight hump in the snow where we'd just buried Campbell.

Even now I still couldn't believe it. I'd heard about such things, of course. Who hasn't? But to actually see it with my own eyes . . .

I suddenly became aware of the cold wind penetrating the thick insulation of my parka and knew we'd have to get back to camp soon before we all got so cold that we'd never warm up again. Even though it was still only late afternoon, the sky was already beginning to darken, the heavy snow clouds bulking up to rob us of even that last, poor vestige of daylight.

I jerked a thumb over my shoulder, pointing the way back to camp just as the day's first flakes of snow began to fall like bleached autumn leaves, and I looked at them at last, waiting for them to begin the awkward, thirty-yard march back to the clearing amid the stunted spruces where we'd pitched our tents, but none of them moved.

For one awful moment I wondered if they'd all frozen to death while I'd been stumbling over the few meaningless phrases with which we'd buried Campbell. They stood around the grave like a trio of bizarre statues, their eyes hidden behind dark Hoven snow goggles. They could have died there and I wouldn't have known a thing about it. I could be left out here alone —

But then Sherman gave me the thumbs-up and my shoulders dropped with relief. As the icy wind picked up around us, we tramped back to the light and warmth and reality of our camp, hoping vainly to leave some, at least, of the horror behind.

* * *

Back in the main tent we pulled off our caps, goggles, scarves and gloves, and sat in a circle, waiting for Quinlan to brew up some coffee. None of us spoke. None of us so much as *looked* at anyone else.

When the coffee came it was thick and black and just what we needed. We drank in silence, allowing ourselves to thaw out gradually, until Sherman got to his feet and turned up the lamps, and Quinlan lit a cigarette after offering the packet around.

It was then that Weaver spoke, his gentle brown eyes not lifting from the surface of his coffee. 'It's the work of the devil,' he muttered.

Sherman and I exchanged a look as Quinlan leapt up. He and Weaver were almost complete opposites, Quinlan tall, wide and practical, Weaver short, slight, academic.

'That's bullshit,' growled Quinlan.

'Is it?' Weaver countered mildly.

Quinlan fixed Sherman with a hard look. 'Well, what do *you* think?' he demanded. And then, when Sherman made no reply, 'What about you — *Cap*?'

I shrugged. 'I don't know. I — '

'You don't *know*?' Quinlan gave a snort, and not for the first time I found myself wondering just who was really supposed to be in charge of this crew. 'Haven't you fucks ever heard of spontaneous combustion? Spontaneous *human* combustion? What about that guy in Michigan, back in the fifties? You must've heard about *that!* Just went up, *whoosh*, right behind the wheel of his car.'

'I've heard about it,' I said. 'But — '

'Out *here*?' asked Weaver, his pale skin stretched tight across his narrow face. 'With the temperature at twenty below?'

Quinlan drew angrily on his cigarette. Beneath the light of the lamp his face looked even ruddier than usual. It gave him an almost demonic appearance. 'You're all scared, that's your trouble.'

Sherman looked at him, and I could

see my own fear mirrored in his pale grey eyes. 'Can you blame us?' he asked. 'After all that's happened?'

Quinlan ignored him, taking great pains to crush his cigarette thoroughly on the sole of one large boot before looking at each of us in turn. 'You're all scared,' he said again, as his eyes came to rest on me.

I finished my coffee slowly, not because I wanted it but because it was better than having to argue with Quinlan. I knew that as leader it was up to me to decide what we should so, but I was fresh out of ideas. If we could have taken a radio with us, or a cell phone, I could have asked for someone to tell *me* what to do. But out here, in the heart of the Katmai National Monument, radios and cell phones were useless, surrounded as we were by high mountains and adverse weather conditions.

In any case, why couldn't Quinlan *understand* our fear? We'd all seen Campbell's blackened corpse out there in the snow. I had even seen the flames that had eaten at his writhing body. But it wasn't just Campbell's death that had us all spooked. There was more to it than that.

Six of us had made the 230-mile flight from Anchorage to the cluster of sturdy log cabins known as Kelsey's Point. Six of us had been met there by Quinlan, who had been hired to act as our guide on the sixty-mile trek into the wilderness of the national park about which we had come to make our documentary.

But then, three days ago, McVeigh had disappeared.

We'd searched all over for him, but found nothing to tell us where he'd gone or what had happened to him, not even so much as a single footprint. Quinlan had suggested that he might have been attacked by a wolf-pack or a bear. Such things weren't exactly unheard-of in this Godforsaken part of Alaska. Indeed, the wildlife that lived here undisturbed was one of the principal things we'd wanted to feature in our film.

After that we started carrying rifles. Oh, the faith we'd had in those rifles! That was, until Linaker went missing, and

Campbell found a puddle of bubbling fat in the snow just twenty yards west of camp.

Even then we didn't connect the two events. Out in the middle of country as rough as this you have to expect casualties: that's why it's so hard for people like us to get insurance.

It wasn't until Campbell died that we realised something was terribly wrong, and now that we knew it, I couldn't decide what the hell we should do about it.

There was probably a rational explanation for what had happened to McVeigh and Linaker. But what if there *wasn't*? What if their disappearances were connected in some way to Campbell's death? Were we all sitting here over-reacting simply because we were stuck out in the middle of nowhere, or —

'It's the work of the devil,' Weaver said again.

We sat around in our circle, avoiding each other's eyes again for what felt like an eternity. Then Sherman said, 'What'll we do, then, Cap?'

He was a tall, athletic man in his early

thirties, and one of the best wildlife cameramen I'd ever worked with, but as I looked into his eyes now all I could see was desperation. He and Weaver were two of a kind. When the going got rough they needed someone else to take charge and tell them what to do.

I should have pitied them, really, sitting forward anxiously to catch my every word, but instead I hated them, because although they were scared, I figured I was more scared than the pair of them put together.

'We're leaving,' I said briefly. I didn't look at Quinlan, but busied myself reaching for a cigarette of my own.

'We're running away,' Quinlan said softly.

I had to look at him then, and when our eyes met it was hard not to look away. 'We're *leaving*,' I repeated, forcing some iron into my tone. 'There's a difference.'

'Not as far as I can see.'

'Well, if you've got any better ideas, why not share 'em around? What do *you* think we should do, carry on trying to shoot this fucking film and hope we don't all go up the same way Campbell did?'

Quinlan made a brief gesture of dismissal with his left hand. 'That was a fluke, like I said. Spontaneous combustion.'

'What about the others?'

His eyes slid away from mine and I felt an absurd sense of triumph, as if I'd beaten him in some way. 'That was just coincidence,' he replied after a moment. 'They strayed too far from camp, most likely got lost or attacked by — '

' — a wolf-pack or a bear,' I cut in. It wasn't hard to lock eyes with him now, because I was supposed to be in charge of this merry little band and ever since we'd started out, Quinlan had done nothing but try to undermine my authority.

He was supposed to be our combination guide and script consultant, a job at which he was completely professional. But away from it he had a habit of comparing everyone to himself, and if they didn't match up — which of course none of us L.A. types had — he treated them like dirt.

I leaned towards him and said, 'I

don't think you understand just how serious this is, Quinlan. Three men are *dead*. Dead! Three men who came here to shoot a documentary, not get themselves killed!'

The silence was so thick after my outburst that you could have cut it with Quinlan's Spyderco rescue knife. I glared at him, just daring him to open that fat mouth of his again.

He did.

'We don't know the other two are dead,' he growled. 'Don't forget, Cap, I *know* this country.'

Before I could respond, Sherman stepped between us. 'Ah, shut up, Quinlan. They're dead, all right.'

His voice caught a little as he said it.

'We're leaving, and that's all there is to it.'

I let my breath out in a soft rush, glad to have had some support. I was so angry that I couldn't trust myself to speak right away, but after a moment I cleared my throat and said, 'All right, chill, everyone. It's too late to do anything now, so try to get some sleep.

We'll pull out at first light tomorrow.'

I glanced at Quinlan for agreement.

'Yes, *sir*,' he said, slicing the air with a vicious mock salute. He tugged on his cap, goggles and gloves and left, heading for the low-profile tent he'd been sharing with Weaver. It was full dark out now, and the snow was still falling.

'He's a bastard,' Sherman muttered, shaking his head.

I blew smoke toward the ceiling of the tent. 'I know. Trouble is, right now we can't afford to be enemies. Without him, we're *lost* out here.'

* * *

I don't suppose any of us expected to sleep much that night, but at least in sleep there was some respite from this mess. I lay quietly in my sleeping bag, running the events of the last few days through my mind, but nothing seemed to make sense. Outside, the wind whipped through the trees and a stray draught made the flame of my lamp flicker. I felt more alone then than I'd ever done before, and wished I were sharing with one of the others. But since Linaker had gone, I'd had the tent to myself.

Tomorrow we faced a sixty-mile journey over some of the roughest terrain in the world. With luck, we could be back at Kelsey's Point within five days, maybe a little less if we had good weather. But if anything should happen to Quinlan, we were completely cut off from the outside world.

I turned onto my side and closed my eyes. I'd pinned everything on this film. After three years of producing and directing documentaries on a whole variety of subjects, I'd decided that this one was finally going to put me on the map. This one was going to win me a clutch of awards and help me take a step up to one of the big networks. I hadn't figured on it ending like this.

I guess I must have drifted off to sleep sometime after midnight, trying not to think about Campbell but seeing over and over again in my mind the awful, gut-twisting manner of his death.

Which was strange, really, because I

didn't actually see how it came to happen at all. None of us did. We'd all been busy with our own tasks, still secretly speculating on the fates of McVeigh and Linaker when suddenly, above the constant moan of the wind there came a kind of deep, dull *whoomp* of sound and a wave of hot air pushed me forward.

My first thought was for Campbell, who'd been ten or twelve feet behind me, sorting out cables for the lights, but when I turned around to see what had happened, he was nowhere in sight.

Instead, my attention was taken by a bright orange flame that rose up out of the ground to a height of about eight feet.

Out here, in the middle of all this snow and ice, it looked so incongruous, that flame that shot up from out of a puddle of melted snow. My mind started screaming questions, demanding to know what the fuck was going on, but then all thought was wiped from my mind as Campbell appeared briefly — *right at the heart of the fire*.

A terrible, numbing dread settled over

me then, as I watched him reaching out to me, his fingers clenching and unclenching in agony.

He took a stumbling step forward, his mouth yanked down at the corners in a scream that was drowned by the crackling flames, and then his legs buckled and he ploughed face-forward into the snow.

He kicked his legs weakly as the flames fed on him, his hands pounding a desperate tattoo in the snow as his screams finally cut through the bitter air.

In seconds he was reduced to little more than a charred black mess. And then the flames began to shrink in size until all that was left were a few glowing embers in the small of his back, and then even they blinked out.

Then it was over.

Smoke rose from the corpse in lazy grey clouds, and I realised that I was whimpering, that I couldn't seem to stop, that the others had rushed up to join me and that Weaver was tearing his scarf loose so that he could throw up in the snow.

That's when I remembered that puddle

of bubbling fat Campbell had found in the snow during our search for Linaker. All at once it took on a terrible significance.

Something awful had started happening to us. But what?

What?

* * *

In the end it was a relief to wake up, or rather, to be *woken* up. When I opened my eyes I found Quinlan crouching over me, one large, calloused hand shaking my shoulder. I blinked a couple of times and tried to paste a smile onto my face, to show him that there were no hard feelings after yesterday's argument.

'Time to pull out,' he said, and I couldn't tell if his voice held a note of sarcasm or not.

I nodded once before he added, 'Sherman's gone.'

At first I didn't understand what he was trying to say. Part of my mind was still asleep, the rest made lazy by the constant, numbing cold.

Then, all at once, it hit me.

'*What?*'

My voice was a crushed whisper.

Quinlan looked toward the tent flap and said, 'You'd better see for yourself.'

I was up and outside with him in less than half a minute. The sky was dull grey and fresh snow clung to the branches of the surrounding spruces. The Malamutes, tethered to an ice-topped length of chain, looked as if they were smiling at the prospect of some exercise, their breath turning to mist in the sharp air. Weaver, standing nearby, was hugging himself to keep warm, his pale, goggle-dotted face turned toward me.

I followed Quinlan across to Sherman's tent, bent and peered inside when the guide opened the flap for me.

The first thing that hit me was the heat — welcome at first, until you caught the smell it carried with it, that acrid, charred stench of something burnt to a cinder.

My eyes pierced the gloom until I saw Sherman's blackened body. He was stretched out on his back, I think, though it was hard to tell since all the recognisable features had been seared away.

I straightened abruptly, turned away and sucked down air that shrivelled my lungs. My heart hammered and my legs threatened to buckle beneath me. All I could think was that Sherman was dead, that he'd died the same way Campbell had, the same way McVeigh and Linaker had, for all we knew.

And while he lay with smoke still curling up from his warm corpse, the tent around him remained *completely untouched*.

3

Just over half an hour later we were ready to go.

We'd arrived with our supplies and equipment evenly distributed over seven sleds, but now we had to load as much as we could onto three and put more dogs into the traces to compensate for the extra weight. I would have preferred to have used snowmobiles, but Quinlan had told us we'd be better off with dogs, which, he'd claimed, were less likely to break down. So dogs it was.

We threw ourselves into the business of packing, intent on keeping ourselves too busy to wonder much about what was happening around us, and we worked in silence until at last we were ready to leave.

Quinlan stood behind his sled, moving from one foot to the other in what I took to be his sudden impatience to get going.

I could hardly blame him for his change of heart.

Weaver, next in line, was still hugging himself in an effort to stop shivering. What little skin I could see between his goggles and scarf looked grey. He appeared to be watching something to the north, but when I followed his line of vision I couldn't see anything.

As I took up position behind my own sled, I paused for one last look around the clearing to which we'd come just under a week earlier. There'd been seven of us then: now we were down to three.

A grebe hopped from one snowy branch to another, its head tilted to one side as if it didn't quite know what to make of us.

Again I thought, *I didn't figure on it ending like this*.

I gave Quinlan the thumbs-up and he nodded before turning to face forward again.

'*Hi!*'

His command didn't echo across the plain, but rather was swallowed by the silence that surrounded us. His sled began to move, slowly at first, then with gathering speed, Weaver's following close behind in fits and starts. Poor old Weaver: he never had gotten the hang of handling the dogs.

I brought up the rear, my thick-gloved hands clutching the handrail awkwardly.

After a while it felt good to be moving, to feel the sharp air tightening my skin and see the muscular bodies of the Malamutes straining in the traces. But more than that, it felt good to be leaving that clearing and its awful memories.

* * *

The winters in that part of the world are nine months long, and even in summer the days are bitingly cold. The temperature hovered around freezing all day, and not even the effort of driving the sleds could warm us up much. At midday we stopped to melt some snow for coffee, sheltering from the wind behind a wide needle of rock that had been thrust up from the earth during some past volcanic activity.

The coffee warmed us from the inside out, and as I drank I watched the dogs, biting at the snow to moisten their mouths and admired their stamina. Personally, I felt shattered, both mentally and physically, but I knew we had to keep going. There was no choice, not if we wanted to survive.

It was at that moment that I glanced at Weaver, who still appeared to be watching something along our back-trail. Again I followed his line of vision, again saw nothing but a great field of snow, unbroken save for an occasional grey boulder or stand of stunted trees.

He studied the terrain with an intensity I hadn't thought him capable of, until I asked quietly, 'All right, Jeff?'

He blinked a couple of times, then turned to me, offering a brief tic of a smile before finishing his coffee.

I glanced out over the plain. 'See something?'

'No, nothing. Imagination, I guess.'

I studied him briefly before returning my gaze to the plain. '*Sure?*'

'Sure.'

Quinlan finished checking on the dogs, straightened up and motioned us back to our positions. We marched back to our sleds without another word. The mountains loomed jaggedly before us, their bases shrouded in a fine, clinging mist. There was nothing beautiful about them, although once I might have thought so. Now they were merely obstacles that stood between us and safety: obstacles to be overcome.

As we moved off, I had to fight the urge to look behind me again. I knew there was nothing there, and yet I still saw the intense, tight-lipped concentration on Weaver's face as he had studied . . . *what?*

My skin began to crawl, as if alien eyes were watching me from the cover of the trees. I knew it was only my imagination, but . . .

But . . .

⋆ ⋆ ⋆

By late afternoon the sky had clouded over and snow began to fall in a steady white sheet.

Quinlan led us to a stand of misshapen cottonwoods in which we pitched the largest tent. We hadn't previously discussed sleeping arrangements, but I knew none of us wanted to spend the night alone. We all knew that, if something should happen to one of us, at least the other two would be on hand to help him — if help were at all possible.

By full dark we were sitting inside the tent, drinking a concoction Quinlan called Russian tea. It tasted of many things, especially cloves and whiskey, and if I'd been anywhere else I probably would have poured it away. But out in the middle of that wasteland it was as welcome as a hearty meal and a roaring fire.

A roaring fire . . .

I shuddered.

When Quinlan returned from feeding the dogs, Weaver and I dished up a thick broth we'd boiled in the can. As we sat spooning the soup, I knew we were all secretly feeling pretty pleased with ourselves. The going had been rough but the progress fair. We reckoned to have made about nine miles that day.

We were very careful not to discuss the reason for our flight, as if by talking about it we might invite it into the tent with us. Instead, we talked about general topics. That is to say, Quinlan and I did. Weaver didn't say much at all.

I glanced at him from time to time but I don't think he was even listening to us. His eyes were on the tent flap, and he appeared to be listening to — or *for* — something outside. I considered asking him about it, but to do so would mean breaking our unspoken agreement to not even *mention* it. I know Quinlan was watching him, but he too refrained from comment.

For his part, Quinlan was certainly in a more congenial mood, and in spite of our present situation it was fascinating to listen to him talking about this land and the wildlife that abounded there.

I knew that he'd felt cheated when his first chance to work on a TV show had turned sour, but whether he cared to admit it or not, I think Sherman's death had finally impressed upon him our need to retreat, and I was glad he was with us now, instead of against us.

It had been a hard day, and though we were reluctant to surrender to sleep, eventually we could no longer keep our eyes open. I asked Quinlan if we should take turns keeping watch (an idea Weaver was all for), but he didn't think it was necessary, and I was too tired to argue the point. By nine-thirty we were all asleep.

* * *

Just to have survived the night was a shot in the arm for us, and when we woke the following morning I was pleased to see that even Weaver's mood had lightened.

We set off just as the weak orange sun started burning the last of the night's mist from the snowy ground, and stopped once before noon when Quinlan saw some tracks off to our left. While he checked them out, I took the opportunity to exchange a few words with Weaver, generalities really, just to see how much he really *had* loosened up.

A few minutes later we watched

Quinlan stamp back towards us, the air escaping from between his bewhiskered lips in great, steaming clouds. 'It's all right,' he said, taking up position behind his own sled again. 'I wasn't sure what they were at first, but they're wolf tracks. A pack of about thirteen, I'd say.'

Weaver and I looked again at the churned-up snow twenty yards from where we stood. Even to our inexperienced eyes it was obvious that a struggle of some sort had taken place, but we couldn't understand the significance of several white sticks or branches that were scattered nearby. Weaver asked Quinlan about them, and an uncharacteristic smile creased the guide's weathered face.

'They must've come across a dead or dying moose,' he explained. 'Those 'sticks' are its bones. Wolves picked 'em clean.'

As we moved off, I wondered if that's what had happened to Linaker and McVeigh. If you ignored the pool of bubbling fat that Campbell had found — which was no evidence at all, really — then all we had were a lot of wild guesses about what had happened to them. Was it possible that they *had* strayed, as Quinlan had suggested, and been attacked the way the moose had? But if that were the case, why hadn't we found *their* bones?

The ground was sloping steadily upward now, and the dogs had to lean fully into the traces to keep hauling us along. At one point Weaver's sled over-balanced and he fell heavily into a snow drift. By the time we had got everything sorted out again, Quinlan decided to call a halt, and Weaver and I pestered him to brew up some more Russian tea.

While he busied himself with the request, I checked on the dogs, searching for any who might have been injured in the fall or sickening for something, but found them all in good shape and keen to get moving again.

A light snow began to powder my shoulders, turning steadily heavier as I returned to the shelter of the rocks in which Quinlan had set up our temporary camp. As I came in, Quinlan said, 'You'd better tell Weaver it's ready.'

I glanced around. The snow was falling pretty thickly now and I couldn't see Weaver anywhere. 'Where did he go?' I asked.

Quinlan shrugged. 'I thought he was taking a leak.'

I shivered, trying to fight the panic that rose within me, and took a couple of steps back the way I'd just come. '*Weaver!*'

My cry was torn away by the wind.

'*Weaver!*'

We waited.

There was no answer.

I realised then that Quinlan had joined me, and when I glanced at him I was surprised to see concern stamped across his weathered features.

We didn't say anything, but we were both thinking the same thing: that if Weaver had wandered too far in this snowstorm he might get lost or attacked by half-starved animals, or —

Or he might ignite.

Christ.

'*Weaver!*'

The snow was biting into my face now,

great flakes of it hammering into the ground as if each piece weighed a ton. Quinlan yelled Weaver's name, but still there was no reply.

'What do you suppose — ?'

I shrugged. 'Christ knows. *Weaver!*'

And then we saw him about thirty feet away, a dark figure almost hidden by the wall of snow. But even as relief flushed through me, I noticed that he was staggering, as if he were trying to run, and the panic surged back. Something was wrong.

Quinlan pushed past me and loped out to meet him. Weaver fell against him and Quinlan had to half-drag him back to where the fire spluttered gamely against the snapping wind. Without a word Quinlan poured some Russian tea and forced it down Weaver's throat. Weaver choked at first, but then began to swallow. He looked as pale as the snow around us, his haunted eyes made darker by the grey rings that ate into the skin beneath them.

'What is it?' I asked. 'What's wrong?'

Weaver's eyes were rolling, his fingers, now reaching for the mug in Quinlan's hand, trembling visibly. Ignoring the heat, he emptied the contents of the mug down his throat, spilling thin trickles down either side of his mouth, where they crusted to ice even as I watched.

'Weaver, what *is* it?'

Then all movement in him stopped, and I thought he was dead. But after a second he turned those dark eyes on me and they made me feel colder than any snowstorm. The colour started coming back into his pale face. He lifted one hand and pointed a steady, gloved finger back the way he'd come, then nodded to himself, twice.

'Over there . . . ' he said in a near whisper. 'A large . . . rock . . . sh-shaped like . . . a . . . fist . . . '

'What about it?' I yelled above the wind.

Weaver's eyes widened again. '*Footprints!*' he managed in a strangled voice. 'Just like I . . . thought. We're not *alone* out here, Cap! We're being *followed!*'

* * *

The dogs howled as the storm continued to lash at us with its cold fury. Weaver led the way and Quinlan and I followed, not sure what to expect. In his large hands Quinlan held a rifle wrapped in animal skin, and while its presence seemed to comfort Weaver, it made me feel more nervous than I had all the way through this ordeal.

The wind burned our skin and stole our breath as we struggled forward across the uneven ground. If Weaver was right, and someone *had* been following us, who was he, and why hadn't he made his presence known? Even as we approached the rock Weaver had described, I wondered if we were finally going to solve this mystery.

As if on cue, the wind began to die down, the snow to thin a little. Over the years, the weather had eaten into the rock so now it had the appearance of a huge fist, knuckles and all. As we stood looking at it, the dogs gradually calmed until the silence that followed was near-absolute.

'Well?' asked Quinlan.

Weaver was looking at the ground. 'Here,' he pronounced after a moment. 'I was just walking around, and I saw them. Here.'

We looked at the ground but there was nothing to see but smooth snow. Weaver fell to his knees, his head moving in small, urgent movements as he scanned the ground. 'They were *here*,' he insisted. 'They were as real as the prints we've just left behind us.'

He turned to look up at me, and the pleading in his face made me look away from him. He climbed awkwardly back to his feet. 'Oh, come *on*, Cap, don't look like that! I'm not imagining it! They were real!'

You could hear the desperation in the strangled pitch of his voice. I didn't know what to say, but if I told him he was just imagining things it might push him over the edge.

After a moment I said, 'Maybe there *were* some tracks. They could've been hidden by that last snowfall.'

Before Weaver could reply, Quinlan said, 'There *were* tracks.'

Weaver smiled in triumph. 'You see? What did I tell you?'

'They were *yours*,' Quinlan told him harshly. He jabbed a finger at the ground. 'See 'em? Look closely at those faint bumps in the snow. That's where your tracks were filled in by that last fall.'

I saw them, then, vague boot-prints that you could just about follow back the way we'd come, slightly raised from the rest of the snow so that they cast very faint but undeniable shadows.

There was only one set of tracks.

'I *saw* them,' Weaver insisted. He looked from Quinlan to me, a faint sheen of what could have been ice or sweat across his forehead. 'Well, what is it, then? You think I'm crazy, or what?'

'We didn't say that,' I told him.

'Look, Weaver, it's easy to imagine — '

Weaver turned his back on us. 'I didn't imagine anything,' he said coldly. When he turned back to us I thought I saw tears glistening in his eyes. 'Shall we get moving again? We could make another couple of miles this afternoon, eh, Quinlan?'

He strode off without waiting for a reply.

* * *

The following day we woke to a clear blue sky. There was no change in the temperature, but with the promise of good weather Quinlan was confident that we might make as many as ten or twelve miles if we pushed ourselves and the dogs.

Ten or twelve miles . . . my mouth almost watered at the prospect. If you added that to the nine miles we'd made on the first day and the eight we'd made on the second, that made twenty-eight miles. Twenty-eight miles between us and that cursed clearing amid the spruces! And only another thirty-some miles to civilisation.

We packed the tent away in silence, each of us busy with our own appointed tasks, and with our shadows stretched powder-blue across the snow by the early morning sun, we moved on.

That day went much like the previous

two. We slipped across great fields of snow, each of us alone with his thoughts, and trying to keep his sled from over-balancing and holding the others up. The snow was broken here and there by scattered patches of hardy scrub, trees and boulders, but anything further than a mile away was lost in a blur of fine, cold mist.

By now we were beginning to look more like animals than men, with our hair growing shaggy and untrimmed beards shading our chins. We felt grimy, our unwashed bodies enclosed in the same unwashed clothes, but on a day such as this, with the dogs pulling us yard after yard closer to Kelsey's Point, our spirits were probably at their highest.

All except for Weaver, that was. He had hardly spoken since the footprint business of the previous afternoon, and had retired to his sleeping bag as soon as we'd finished our evening meal, whether to sleep or not, I couldn't say. I only knew that he was the first of us up the following morning, his eyes dull and bloodshot, his mouth a tight line of ill temper.

We stopped briefly at noon to rest the dogs and warm ourselves with coffee. We didn't speak much and were off again before twenty minutes had passed.

Toward the end of the day, as the sun began to sink and stretch our shadows again, my spirits dropped a little. It had been a beautiful day, we'd made a surprising and gratifying twelve miles and I was reluctant for it to end. But as the sky began to darken we made for a stand of cedars where we pitched our tent and prepared for the coming evening. By the time the moon had risen, the dogs had been fed and we were safely installed under canvas.

We were all pretty tired and the comparative warmth of the tent made us feel even drowsier. We sat together in an atmosphere not entirely comfortable, since Weaver's continued silence seemed to radiate hostility. He was still showing off, and though I felt sorry for him, I wasn't going to worry about him any more than I had to. Out of the seven of us, he was the one least suited to the outdoor life, and the events of the past week had been hard on him, but we were all in the same boat now.

I was just dozing off when Weaver said, 'Why?'

As I opened my eyes, Quinlan asked, 'Why what?'

Weaver was sitting opposite me, his thin legs crossed. He leaned forward, a too-bright light showing in his eyes. 'Well, we were all so scared after Campbell and Sherman went up that we just decided to run. We didn't stop to ask *why* it happened.'

'It happened,' Quinlan stated flatly. 'That was enough.'

Weaver put his hands up, showing blistered palms. 'Oh, don't get me wrong. I was all for leaving. But have you given it any thought since? *Why* it happened?'

I was tired and I wanted to go to sleep. But irritably I admitted, 'I've hardly thought about anything else.'

'And?'

'And I haven't got a clue,' I replied.

Weaver gave an annoying little snicker. 'Oh, come on, Cap, you must have. Even if it's just a half-assed theory, let's hear it.'

'I haven't even got a half-assed theory,' I replied. 'But I get the feeling *you* do.'

He inclined his head. 'I've got an idea, sure,' he confessed. He was quiet for a moment, possibly for effect. Then he said, 'Although Katmai's a national monument, it's still largely unexplored, right?'

Quinlan nodded cautiously.

'Well, suppose the land itself wanted it *kept* that way?'

'I don't follow.'

'Any film we made about this area, any exposure we gave it, would inevitably draw people to the region to find out more,' Weaver explained. 'Maybe only a few at first, but over time in increasing numbers. Cartographers, surveyors, naturalists, speculators, tourists, park rangers.'

He was leaning so far forward now that I thought he was going to overbalance.

'What's your point?' growled Quinlan.

'Suppose there was something, I don't know what, let's say something in the land *itself*, that didn't want that to happen? Something that just wanted this region to stay as isolated and unspoiled as it is right now. How do you suppose it would achieve that?'

Quinlan shook his head. 'Tell us,' he invited coolly.

Weaver did.

'By killing off the very people who were going to make that film in the first place and give it all that free publicity,' he said.

I snorted. 'That's crazy.'

'Is it, Cap?' he countered. 'Think about it for a minute. This entire region was created by a series of volcanic eruptions. That's *heat*, Cap. Heat and *fire*.'

'It's garbage,' I said.

'It's bullshit,' growled Quinlan, getting to his feet and unrolling his High Peak sleeping bag.

'Bullshit, is it?' Weaver echoed. 'Well, at least it's a theory. If you can come up with a better one, then — '

'Can it, Jeff.'

Weaver flicked an angry glance at me. 'Butt out, Cap. I'm talking to the great scout here — '

Quinlan reached down with a speed that made me flinch and grabbed a handful of Weaver's parka. He hauled

Weaver to his feet and brought back his free hand in a bunched fist.

'*All right,*' I yelled, '*that's enough!*'

Quinlan glanced at me, then back to Weaver. The guide dwarfed him. I got to my feet, ready to step in before it came to blows, but even as I did so, Quinlan released Weaver's parka and pushed him away. He was about to say something, then thought better of it and turned to unzip his sleeping bag.

Weaver stood there with the sweat of fear making his red face glisten. In the sudden silence all that could be heard was his laboured breathing. Abruptly he bent and picked up his gloves. As he headed for the tent flap I asked, 'Where are you going?'

He didn't look at me. 'To take a leak.'

Quinlan muttered, 'It'll freeze before it hits the snow. Use the pot in here.'

Weaver didn't reply, but brushed out of the tent in a quick, angry movement. I looked at the flap for a second before saying, 'Should I go after him?'

Quinlan was climbing into his bag. He shook his head. 'No, he'll be all right. It's a full moon out there, plenty of light. Just let him cool off.'

I cursed. 'What next? Just when you think everything's going okay — '

'It *is* going okay. Another few days like today and we'll have made it.'

'Yeah, but — '

Quinlan sat up, his face serious as he studied me. 'Look, don't worry about Weaver, *or* me. I'm not going to start anything. I just want to get home.'

I busied myself with my own sleeping bag, trying to keep my voice neutral as I asked, 'Do you think there's anything to what he said?'

He grunted. 'What, about the land wanting to stay unspoiled, you mean?'

I nodded.

'Well, what do *you* think?' he asked, closing his eyes and turning onto his side.

I watched him for a while before speaking again. 'It's just that, since we've been on the move, nothing's happened. I mean, we're all still okay.'

'You mean none of us has gone up in flames.'

'Yeah.'

Quinlan rolled onto his back to look up at me again. 'He's crazy, Cap. This business has pushed him over the edge. He'll probably snap out of it once we get back to civilisation, but right now, he's wild.'

He turned onto his side again and after a while I climbed into my own bag and closed my eyes too. About ten minutes later I heard Weaver come back in. I wasn't in any mood for conversation so I just lay there, feigning sleep. I heard Weaver whisper my name but ignored him. A second later I felt his hand on my shoulder, shaking me gently.

I opened my eyes. 'What now?' I asked.

Weaver's face was close to mine, and I could see that mad gleam back in his eyes. 'Someone's outside,' he replied, his voice as soft as my own, but far more urgent.

He saw the look of disbelief wash across my face and added hurriedly, 'It's true, Cap! And I'll tell you something else, too. I know who it is!'

I sat up impatiently. 'All right, all right. Out with it.'

He studied me for a moment before saying, 'It's McVeigh, Cap. It's *McVeigh*.'

* * *

For a moment my mind went blank. I just didn't know what to think. I wanted to dismiss it as another of Weaver's fantasies, but an insistent little voice at the back of my mind kept reminding me that we'd never found anything to prove that McVeigh was dead — not even so much as the puddle of spitting fat we'd found when Linaker disappeared. We'd just assumed . . .

I glanced at Quinlan's still form, reluctant to bring him into the conversation, but even as I studied him he rolled over, looking at us through sleep-narrowed eyes as he demanded to know what we were whispering about.

I looked briefly at Weaver before saying, 'Now listen, Quinlan, don't say anything.' I took a deep breath and let it out in an embarrassed sigh. 'Weaver thinks he's seen McVeigh.'

'I *did* see him,' Weaver objected, looking at Quinlan from beneath cautiously-hooded lids.

I wasn't sure what I expected Quinlan

to do, but to my surprise he didn't let go a stream of abuse. Instead, he merely sat up, unzipped his sleeping bag and reached for his rifle, and with a weary sigh he said, 'Come on, then. Let's take a look.'

* * *

The full moon spread its pale radiance across the plain as we stepped out into the bitter night. The landscape was deathly still and quiet. Blurred patches of darkness showed the position of rocks, trees and bushes: places where a man could hide. But if McVeigh was out there, why should he want to *hide* from us?

'All right, let's hear it,' Quinlan demanded in a whisper. There was an edge to his voice that could have been annoyance with Weaver or just impatience to get back to sleep.

Weaver said, 'I came out here and just started walking. I didn't know or care much about where I was going.' We could see the thin grey line of churned-up snow that marked his trail, leading to a shrub-shaded cluster of boulders about a hundred or more yards from where we stood. 'I was walking so fast that I slipped. That's when I caught a movement out of the corner of my eye. I thought it was a wolf or something. I didn't want to think it was anything else. But then I realised that it was moving on its hind legs. It was a man.'

'Where?'

Weaver indicated the shadowed cluster of rocks. 'Just behind those boulders,' he said.

'What did you do then?' demanded Quinlan.

'I just stood there, watching it.'

'So you didn't make contact with him at all?'

'No.'

'Then how'd you know it was McVeigh?'

'Well, who else could it be out here?'

'Oh, for — '

But Quinlan bit off any further comment. He flicked me a tired look, and holding the rifle across his wide chest he raised his voice. '*McVeigh! Is that you out there?*'

His shout was smothered by the still night air and thrown back in soft echoes that rippled across the snow.

'*McVeigh! Listen, whoever you are, we don't mean you any harm!*'

We waited for the echoes to die, and when we were sure there would be no reply, we began to move forward, Quinlan in the lead, Weaver and I following behind him like obedient sheep.

The snow crushed softly beneath our boots. In the eerie light every shadow seemed to quiver with a life of its own. I glanced at Weaver and the expression on his face left me in no doubt that he really believed that someone was out there.

About halfway to the cluster of boulders we stopped and Quinlan raised his voice again.

'*McVeigh! Anyone! Come out. We're friends!*'

FRIENDS . . . Friends . . . friends . . .

Silence.

After a moment we moved forward again. There was no conversation between us. I threw a glance back at our tent. It looked small and vulnerable there among the trees, and yet when we were inside it we all felt so secure. I shivered. It was pathetic, really, the way I longed for the light and relative warmth of our camp right at that moment.

By the time I faced forward again I was surprised to see that we were almost upon the darkened patch of rocks. Another few slippery steps and we were there. The first thing I looked for were footprints.

There was one set.

Weaver's.

There was nothing else, just undisturbed snow.

We stood side by side for a while, and then, without a word, Quinlan spun on his heel and began to stalk back to camp. There was nothing I could say to Weaver, so I turned and began to follow him. Weaver made no move, but I could feel his eyes burning into my back.

'*I did see someone!*' he screamed at us. '*It was McVeigh! It must have been!*'

I made sure I kept a few paces behind Quinlan, in no hurry to catch up to him until his obvious rage had subsided. Behind me, Weaver yelled, '*He was here!*'

The tent was now less than twenty-five yards away and I longed for the pitiful security it offered more than ever, but at the back of my mind I knew there would be no rest for me unless we were all together. I couldn't just leave Weaver out here alone, no matter how crazy he seemed to be going. Whatever else he was, he was one of us.

I turned and called his name. Beneath the moon's cold glimmer he was a tiny, dejected figure.

'*Come back! I'll prove he was here!*' he shouted, his voice cracked and strained.

'*That's enough, Weaver! Come on, back inside, now!*'

'*But you don't believe me!*' Weaver yelled back.

Behind me, Quinlan swore. 'Come on, Cap. Let him wear himself out. He'll come in when he's cold enough.'

He was probably right. But I had to have one last go. '*Weaver, that's enough! Come on, now!*'

'*No!*'

Quinlan said, 'Leave him, Cap.'

I turned around. 'I guess you're ri — '

And that was when the flame shot up, spurting eight feet into the air like a thing of bright orange liquid, and the incredible blast of heat it produced tore me off my feet.

As the snow burned the skin of my face I heard the bullets in Quinlan's rifle begin to explode as they were detonated by the heat. The crackle of the flames roared in my ears and I buried my face in the snow, ignoring the pain, wanting only to get away from the heat and the screams and the bullets and the terrible knowledge that was being hammered into my skull.

That Quinlan, our guide, had just ignited.

2

And so, it seemed, the worst had happened. The only man who could lead us to safety was dead.

You couldn't really call what we gave him a burial. We shoved snow over the few blackened bits that were left of him and that was that. No meaningless phrases, as I'd called them before, just a hasty, icy shroud of snow.

I felt a lot of things afterwards. Anger, frustration, bitterness. I felt all of those, and more: I felt like getting Weaver and hitting him until his flesh felt more like clammy dough beneath my fists, and at the same time I wanted to take him and look after him because without him I had no-one. I felt betrayal, insecurity, the return of a fear I'd foolishly allowed to diminish with each mile travelled. I felt devastated.

I made my way back to the tent and sat there for a while, listening to the howling of the wind as it began to pick up, feeling my guts quivering as the full significance of Quinlan's death really hit me. *We're stranded*, I told myself over and over. *We're stranded*.

A short time later Weaver joined me. He sat opposite me, fidgeting nervously. His face was stained red from the bite of the wind. I could feel his eyes on me, but I made no attempt to speak to him or even acknowledge his presence. We were stranded. That was all that mattered now. *I* was stranded.

Eventually Weaver broke the silence with a quiet, reasonable question. 'Cap — what are we going to do?'

I looked at him then. And I could only reply, '*I don't know*.'

⋆ ⋆ ⋆

By the time the first grey streaks of dawn were colouring the sky, we were packing the tent and supplies onto our two sleds. All the equipment we had brought with us was stacked beneath two wide canvas sheets further back among the trees. From now on we were moving light and fast: now more than ever it was vital to get back to civilisation.

Going through Quinlan's few possessions a little earlier, I'd found a compass and a couple of dogeared maps. By my reckoning, Kelsey's Point was thirty-five miles to the south and east, but if my calculations were wrong we could find ourselves even worse off than we were already. I asked Weaver to take a look at the maps and let me know what he thought. He was pale and subdued in the morning light, but he was all I had. He studied the maps for a while and when he spoke he confirmed my own conclusions.

We put the strongest of the dogs into the traces and set the rest of them free. When we left the stand of cedars they started to follow us, barking and yapping excitedly as if we were playing a game with them. They stayed with us for an hour or so, until they realised we actually had set them free, then began to veer off in twos and threes and were soon lost to sight. It sounds absurd to say it now, but at the time it felt like losing so many good friends.

The day was cold and the snow was blinding, but thinking back on it, the thing I remember most about it was the fear. It gnawed at my belly like a starving rat. It wasn't the idea of dying that frightened me so much as not knowing when it would happen. Every second of every minute we lived with the knowledge that we might suddenly reach that terrible, mysterious fever pitch and go up, ignite, just like the others had. I found myself praying to God — in whom I had only ever previously half-believed — to save me from the flames. After a while, I chanted the prayer over and over without even thinking about it.

The weather remained dry and under any other circumstances our progress would have been good, but we were forced to make frequent stops to check our course, and scan the terrain for landmarks we could marry up to those on the maps. By the first darkening of the sky we had pitched camp, seen to the dogs and fallen into our sleeping bags. We didn't waste our energy on words: there were no words worth what little energy we had left. We slept from a mixture of exhaustion and nervous reaction. I estimated that we had made a pitiful six miles that first day without Quinlan there to guide us.

⋆ ⋆ ⋆

When I opened my eyes the following morning I became aware of two things. One, that I had survived another night in this wilderness, and two — that I was alone.

Weaver — where was Weaver?

In an instant I was up and tearing the sleeping bag from me. As I barged out of the tent I fully expected to find Weaver's burned body still smouldering in the snow. What I actually saw worried me even more.

He was on his knees, throwing up in the snow.

As I struggled across to him I heard the

little moaning sounds he was making. When he heard me coming, he turned his bloodless face towards me. He looked awful. My first thought was to get him back to the tent, maybe fix him up with a hot drink and some aspirin, but then I stopped, as if my outstretched hand had suddenly hit an invisible barrier.

What if he had something contagious?

'What is it?' I asked.

He swallowed, grimacing at the foulness in his mouth. 'Christ knows,' he managed finally. 'Woke up with it about an hour ago. Nausea, headache . . . had it coming out of both ends.' He swallowed noisily. 'Don't know what it is . . . something I ate, probably. Or something I didn't.'

I nodded, knowing what he meant. For almost a month now we'd been living out of cans, eating — when we could bring ourselves to eat at all — at odd hours and drinking suspect, hastily-boiled coffee. He could be suffering from anything — I just prayed to God that whatever it was, it wouldn't prove fatal.

I waited with him until he felt ready to move, then managed to get him back to the tent. When he was wrapped in his sleeping bag again, I got a little of Quinlan's watered-down whiskey into him. After that he slept for a while, shivering now and then despite the great sea of sweat I wiped from his drawn features every so often.

We stayed where we were for the next two days. I saw to the dogs, constantly foraged for wood to keep our fire burning, slept little and worried much. But finally, the fever broke, and by the end of the second day Weaver could sit up and manage a weak smile of thanks. I almost wept with relief.

Early on the third day, after another long session with the maps, we started off again. By my reckoning, we had approximately twenty-eight miles to cover, and if we didn't start making better time soon, we wouldn't reach Kelsey's Point for another week at least.

⋆ ⋆ ⋆

In the end, however, we did it in four days, although it seemed more like four years. Each hour melted into the next until time lost all meaning for us. We drove ourselves until the last light of day faded from the sky and we could drive ourselves no more. We collapsed into our sleeping bags each night after forcing ourselves to eat and prepare for the following day, and when morning came we were up with the rising sun and driving forward again. We grew light-headed, we saw things in the distance that weren't there at all. Sometimes we would fall asleep whilst driving the sleds and tumble into the snow, not caring if we got up again or not. Each of us kept the other alive, both of us scared that the other would die and leave him here alone. We loved each other, hated each other, we argued, encouraged, berated one another. When two of the dogs died from the unreasonable demands we were making on them, we cried together. We went a little crazy, I guess, out there in a land that could so easily drive men crazy.

But finally, we made it.

There were drifts of snow thirty feet deep all around us and the trail we climbed was so treacherous that our concentration had to be total if we were to travel it successfully. It took us nearly an hour to climb it, and as we reached the top, our lungs screaming for air, the sight of Kelsey's Point — that cluster of sturdy log cabins nestling in a wide valley shielded from the worst of the weather by walls of rock and stands of spruce — took us completely by surprise.

It was still the best part of two miles away, yet crystal clear through the sharp air. As we watched, smoke drifted lazily from one chimney and was snatched away by the chill breeze. I spared a thought for Quinlan and the others and the whole scene misted before my eyes. We'd made it. We'd made it.

After a moment I cleared my throat and, without looking at Weaver, who had gone as completely quiet as I had, said, 'Let's go.'

Weaver's reply was a hearty cry of '*Hi!*' which set the dogs into motion again, hauling our now considerably lightened sleds across that last short distance.

The closer we got to Kelsey's Point, the clearer I could visualise all those things I had grown used to in my life and taken for granted until this moment: of sleeping in a soft bed and eating good, hot food off a clean china plate: the cool satisfaction of a cigarette and being able to relax in a room without draughts: of —

The single street was empty.

We brought our sleds to a halt outside the general store, a single-storey structure combining store, storeroom and living quarters in one. I could just picture the Point's grizzly inhabitants seated around the pot-bellied stove inside, swapping dirty jokes just the way they had when we'd first gone in to purchase our supplies. I thought about sitting around that old stove myself, thawing out for the first time, it seemed, in years.

But the store was empty, too.

We checked the back rooms but found no-one. The stove was cold.

Weaver and I didn't say a word.

We left the general store and went back the way we'd come, to the first of the cabins, the one with the smoke rising from the chimney. I rapped on the door, the sound of knuckles striking wood muffled by my gloves.

We waited for a moment, but there was no answer. I pressed my ear to the door, listened, heard nothing from within. Our eyes met for a moment then, as I grabbed the door handle and pushed. The door was bolted from the inside.

Still not speaking, we trudged around to the side of the cabin to the window. The panes of glass were frosted by the cold. I wiped at one of them, then peered into the single room.

There were four of them inside — about a third of Kelsey Point's population. I couldn't be sure why they'd chosen this cabin to die in, but they were dead all right, their cremated bodies strewn across the bare, unburned boards of the cabin's floor. One of them had fallen half into the fireplace.

I stepped back from the window and looked up, watching the smoke drift high into the air. Weaver peered into the cabin and gave an anguished moan. *No smoke without fire*, I told myself, and gave a crazy little giggle. *No smoke without* . . .

Kelsey's Point had become a graveyard.

* * *

We searched the town and found the others: three men in one cabin, two in another. Three more — the first three to go, I imagined — had been buried behind the general store, their graves marked by simple wooden crosses.

It's a funny thing, really, but just when you receive that final blow, the one that should tear your feet right out from under you, you find some extra reserve of strength and instead of going down you discover that you're able to carry on indefinitely.

That's how it was with us.

Whatever had caused the deaths of our five colleagues had also visited Kelsey's Point, but instead of making us give up there and then, the knowledge made us all the more determined to survive.

Weaver and I moved into the store, which was easy to keep warm and held a large supply of provisions. We stored our equipment — basically the sleds and the rifles — in the cabin next door, which also served as shelter for the dogs. The day after we arrived, we went down to have a look at the airstrip, which was about a hundred and fifty yards east of town. There was a small cabin close by, behind which stood a heavy-duty snow-plough. Inside the cabin were drums of fuel, snowshoes, shovels and picks. There was also a radio set.

To me it was just a mass of knobs and dials, but Weaver said he thought he remembered something about radios from his college days and we spent the next hour trying to contact someone, anyone, on a variety of different frequencies, but all to no avail. A couple of times we picked up the faint promise of a commercial station, all but lost in the crackle of static, but the following day, after a heavy snow-storm, we lost even that.

We waited as patiently as we could for the next two weeks, hoping for contact from the outside world. We tried carefully not to get on each other's nerves, even though any arguments we did have when one or the other of us got a little cranky were soon patched up. In fact, we frequently settled our differences by getting as drunk as we could on the supply of Alaskan Amber we discovered in the cellar.

At times like those, the waiting was almost bearable. Not once did we discuss Quinlan or any of the others, nor did we ever give voice to any more half-assed theories. For my own part, I had given up trying to figure it all out. It had happened, as Quinlan had said, and that was enough.

But I knew it still bothered Weaver. His moods would change with lightning rapidity. Quite often he would go from happy to sad, as quickly as that, and sit for hours staring out across the snowy plain. Tears would roll down his cheeks, but he would make no move to wipe them away, just sit there staring . . .

By the end of the second week the beer was almost gone and what little was left had stopped making us feel good. Our spirits dropped to rock bottom.

But then, three weeks to the day after Quinlan had died, there came proof that we had not been forgotten.

Weaver was out prowling irritably around town and I was stuck in the store, reading a musty old hardcover I'd found somewhere, when I first heard it. I was slumped against the counter and as I put the book down I straightened up, my eyes rolling slowly towards the ceiling. My breathing was shallow, as if I was almost afraid to believe what that faint noise meant. The seconds ticked past and the sound grew louder.

And then I grinned.

In an instant I was around the counter and out into the street, yelling for Weaver.

'*Over here!*' he yelled back.

I turned to face him and could tell by his expression that he had heard it too. The bee-like buzz of a light aircraft engine. A plane!

Together we slipped and slid the distance to the airstrip. I cursed myself for not keeping it ploughed free of snow. Still, if only we could attract the pilot's attention he could always come back for us later.

We came to a halt in the middle of the strip, our breath coming in great white clouds as we scanned the slate grey sky. We'd put on weight since we'd been here, fallen out of condition, and our shoulders rose and fell as we sucked greedily at the air.

That rolling, buzzing sound filled the air now, and Weaver clutched my arm with one hand as he jabbed a finger from the other into the sky.

'*There, Cap! There!*'

We started jumping up and down, yelling and cheering like a couple of kids. The aircraft — a Cessna 350, I thought — was coming in from the south. The pilot waggled his wings to let us know that he'd seen us, and that made us yell and cheer all the harder.

We followed the craft with our eyes as it flew past us, now so low and so close in the clear air that we were able to catch a momentary glimpse into the cockpit.

Then, in an instant, the plane was gone, its wings still waggling as the pilot, his tortured hands still clutching at the controls, writhed in the agony of being burned alive.

Our smiles died.

We could still see the bright orange flames licking at the inside of the cockpit even as the plane disappeared into the north. We stood side by side in silence, watching as it vanished behind the spruces. The cold wind turned our tears to ice.

Four minutes later we heard the plane crash and explode.

* * *

That evening I sat by the stove listening to Weaver's muffled sobs coming from the other room. Snowflakes pattered gently at the windows, driven by a harsh northerly wind. I was still numbed by the shock, but determined not to give up hope. After all, that plane had been sent out here for a reason. When it failed to return, another would come. We would be rescued sooner or later, I felt sure.

My book lay open on my lap. I'd read the same page about four times but hadn't been able to take it in. I sat listening to Weaver for a minute more, then stood up and went in to him, tapping gently on the door before I entered.

He was sitting beside the table, his head in his hands. The room was plain and furnished only with necessities — a bed, a set of drawers, a table and two chairs. A single candle burned in the centre of the table, making our shadows shiver on the bare wooden walls. Weaver didn't look up when I took a seat opposite him.

I wasn't sure what to say to him, so I said nothing. I just sat there, trying to let him know by my very presence that he wasn't alone, that we were both in this together. It could have been worse, I told myself. At least we still had each other. I tried to communicate all this to him just by sitting with him on the other side of the candle. I could tell by the way he sagged in his chair that I didn't succeed.

After a while I said, 'Tomorrow I'm going to plough that runway.'

He made no reply, didn't even spare me a glance.

'I'm going to get it ready for the next plane,' I said.

At last he moved. He looked up at me

and I was surprised and a little hurt to see the hostility in his bloodshot eyes. He shook his head as if in amazement.

'We're as good as dead, Cap,' he murmured thickly. 'Can't you see that?'

'I — '

His face pinched into a frown. 'Oh, save it, Cap. I'm not in the mood for one of your speeches.'

'Listen, I only — '

'I know. You only want to tell me it's all going to be all right, that you've got this feeling about it.' He shook his head savagely, sniffing wetly as he did so. 'Well, I *haven't*.'

I studied the grain on the wooden table top.

'There's no hope left, Cap,' he concluded in a softer tone. 'Don't you *see*? Can't you understand that we're as good as *dead*?'

⋆ ⋆ ⋆

That night I slept but didn't rest. My dreams were vivid and violent but I couldn't remember a single thing about them when I snapped awake at dawn. All was confusion in my mind as I lay there. My heart was pounding and I was breathing hard. My forehead was covered in sweat.

Was this how it began, the build-up to the fever pitch? The thought made my heart race even faster. I forced myself to lay quite still, waiting. I was wheezing like an old man. I felt the pulses throbbing in my temples, nerves twitching in my stomach. Gradually, I calmed down a little. Outside, I could hear the wind howling through the valley, carrying on it the baying of the dogs in the cabin next door.

I sat up, wincing at the pain in the small of my back where I must have slept awkwardly. I ran my fingers through my hair and beard, cursing the dogs for yapping and howling and waking me up so suddenly.

Then, realising how unusual it was for them to act like that, I decided I'd better go take a look around, make sure everything was okay. I got to my feet, shucked into my coat and gloves and left the store, moving quietly so's not to disturb Weaver, whom I had left in the other room last night.

As I stepped out onto the single street I paused to allow myself a yawn and a shiver. Out here the cold wind helped to wake me up. I scanned the empty slopes, saw nothing unusual. And yet I couldn't shake the feeling that something was wrong.

And then I had it.

I hadn't heard it inside, but out here the wind still whipped an echo back from the valley walls, the echo of the sound that had woken me up.

The echo of a gunshot.

I slipped through the snow toward the cabin where the dogs were still howling like mad. I felt the cold morning air stretching the skin of my face as I yelled Weaver's name. I grabbed the door handle, twisted it and threw open the door.

Weaver was sprawled on his back and most of his face had been blown away. One of the rifles lay smoking by his side.

1

And that, basically, is the story.

Three weeks have passed since Weaver committed suicide. Since then I've read that musty old hardcover twice. I taught myself to drive the snowplough and keep the airstrip clear, even though I haven't seen any more planes. And of course I've written this account, partly to record what happened to us, partly to occupy my lonely evenings.

Every day I visit Weaver's grave, which is out behind the store. Sometimes, if the weather's good, I sit and talk to him for hours. I tell him about this and that, how I'm keeping, that the supplies are beginning to run low and that I'm having to go farther afield for firewood.

I haven't been sleeping too well these past few nights. One night last week I thought I heard someone prowling around outside the store, but when I went out the following morning I couldn't find any tracks.

Sometimes I hear voices, people calling me as if from a great distance, but when I search the surrounding slopes, I never see anyone. It sounds terrible to say it, but I think I'm going mad.

If this were a work of fiction, I could probably give you a neat little explanation for why these events occurred. But it isn't fiction. I haven't got any answers, although sometimes I wonder if Weaver could have been right when he said that this land was the cause of it all. Perhaps it *does* want to stay unspoiled, and is protecting itself.

Who can say?

And yet the craziest thing of all is that I still have hope. I still believe that someone, somewhere, is coming to my rescue, so there'll be none of that suicide business for me. I haven't got the guts for it, for one thing. And besides, there's always hope.

There's always

0

Other titles in the Linford Mystery Library:

THE FLUTTERING

David Whitehead

Something terrifying has started happening in Eggerton. People are turning up drained of blood and very, very dead. Have vampire bats started attacking humans? If so, then who's delivering the hammer-blow that finally kills the victims? For Detective Inspector Jack Sears it's a mystery that not even virologist Doctor Christopher Deacon can fathom. But then the police get lucky. Against all the odds one of the victims survives. But strangely enough, that's when things go from bad to worse . . .

DARK LEGION

John Glasby

Near the village of Tormount, on Cranston's Hill, Malcolm Amberley had been found dead. He was discovered in the centre of the Standing Stones, clutching the curiously ornamented hilt of a strange dagger, driven into his heart. A curtain of evil hung over the village, a nightmare for Terence Amberley who arrived to attend his brother's funeral. Did Malcolm commit suicide, or did some evil force still remain viable in the area, forcing him towards a mysterious death?

FEDERAL AGENT

Gordon Landsborough

When Inspector Charlie Chey leads the F.B.I. operation to capture the notorious gunman Red Heydendahl, Charlie is gravely wounded and Red is shot dead in the ensuing battle. Criminals, watching the fighting, mistake Charlie for Heydendahl and rescue him, then take him into hiding for medical attention. But how long will it be before the criminals realise their mistake and discover that they've saved the wrong man? And for Red, their vengeance will be swift and terrible . . .

PATTERN OF MURDER

John Russell Fearn

For cinema projectionist Sid Elbridge, it seems that things can't get any worse. First, circumstantial evidence has made him a police suspect in their investigation into a robbery at the cinema where he works. Next, his fiancée Vera is horribly killed in the same cinema, the victim of a falling light fixture. When Sid accidentally finds strange, intricate patterns traced in the dust on the wooden frame of a still case, his curious discovery will reveal a ruthless murderer . . .

SANDS OF DESTINY

E. C. Tubb

In Africa the Foreign Legion stands between the tribesmen with their dreams of the Great Jehad, and the traders and colonists of the peaceful settlements. Secret agent Lieutenant Crispin de Corville discovers a treacherous plot to unite the tribes and wrest arms from the Legion. Fighting his way across the desert, Corville, while in disguise, must learn the tribesmen's plans as he conveys two women to safety . . . realising that the sands of the desert are indeed the 'Sands of Destiny'.

THE WHEEL SPINS THIRTEEN

John Glasby

In Sharky Dexter's casino in Los Angeles, a man beats the crooked roulette wheel. He places a large bet on number thirteen, which comes up. He lets it ride for a second time and wins again, then stakes the lot on thirteen again — and calmly walks out with a million dollars of winnings! When Sharky hires Johnny Merak to find the man who's taken his money, there's a spate of murders — with Johnny himself a candidate for death . . .